Such an Odd Word to Use

*Uncorrected Proofs
For Review Purposes Only*

Such an Odd Word to Use

CARL GOODWIN

First published in 2025 by
Carl Goodwin, in partnership with Whitefox Publishing Limited

Find out more about Carl Goodwin:

carlgoodwin.com

Copyright © Carl Goodwin, 2025

EU GPSR Authorised Representative
LOGOS EUROPE, 9 rue Nicolas Poussin, 17000, LA ROCHELLE, France
E-mail: Contact@logoseurope.eu

ISBN 978-1-9175236-2-2
Also available as an eBook
ISBN 978-1-9175236-3-9

Carl Goodwin asserts the moral right to be identified as the author of this work.

This is a work of fiction. All characters, organisations and events portrayed in this novella are either products of the author's imagination or are used fictitiously.

All rights reserved. No part of this publication may be reproduced, stored in a retrieval system or transmitted in any form or by any means, electronic, mechanical, photocopying, recording or otherwise, without prior written permission of the author.

While every effort has been made to trace the owners of copyright material reproduced herein, the author would like to apologise for any omissions and will be pleased to incorporate missing acknowledgements in any future editions.

Edited by Kay Coleman and Emily Reader
Designed and typeset by Typo•glyphix
Cover design by Dan Mogford
Project management by Whitefox Publishing Limited
www.wearewhitefox.com

For Melissa (1995–2007)
Whose pencils and papers coloured the world
in ways still felt upon these pages.

Disclaimer

This is a work of fiction inspired by true events. Characters, names, locations, events and incidents are the products of the author's imagination and have been imagined or invented for purposes of dramatisation. Any resemblance to real persons, living or dead, is purely coincidental.

Prologue

It began with Lana asking a simple question from her upstairs window:

'Do you know how to draw rooftops from above?'

I was in the garden, trimming back a climbing vine. I shielded my eyes from the sun and looked up.

'Not especially,' I called back, 'but I imagine squares and rectangles are a good start.'

She gave a thoughtful nod. 'That's what I thought too.'

Only later would I realise this was part of a much larger undertaking – a hand-drawn, heavily annotated map of the neighbourhood, compiled by Lana over the course of a year. A map whose symbols, borders, and colour codes revealed more than one might expect from a child's drawing. It wasn't just a creative pastime – it was an act of deep, almost forensic observation.

Chapter 1

Flickering Light

I should like you to call me Mark. The story I wish to tell all but demands it.

I have no difficulty pinpointing its beginning – it came shortly after I moved into my new home. And so, the days leading up to my first encounter with Alistair are where I shall begin.

♪

I left the house for a routine visit to the gym – a short walk – and returned straight afterwards. No detours – so, all told, probably no more than an hour and a half. Three steps led up to the Georgian entrance – its racing green six-panelled door framed by fluted pilasters and crowned with a sunburst-etched fanlight. Inside, a narrow hallway stretched ahead, lit by the soft echo of daylight from the rear.

On the rainiest days, I sometimes took this more involved route – up the front steps, unlocking the main door, through the hallway, then down a short flight of internal steps to the rear door, which also required unlocking and, once passed through, shutting properly. But today – as on most days – I chose the simpler route: the unsheltered end-of-terrace side access. It led me directly to the communal garden – calm, lightly overgrown, with the hushed feel of a small, half-forgotten woodland. A place the formal Georgian entrance gave no hint of, as if the city had overlooked this one secreted-away patch and let it be. At the far end stood my small, detached house – its lead-grey acoustic front door a soft reminder of the structure's past.

The place still felt unfamiliar, and I could not help but pause for a moment on entering the garden. After years of living in flats that felt more like numbered compartments in a concrete hive, seeing the outer envelope of my home, modest though it was, gave me a thrill – as it might any man in his late thirties finally afforded a little breathing space.

It hadn't been easy to come by.

My love for the novels of Charles Dickens and his larger-than-life characters was what had drawn me to this area. In fact, ever since childhood, my favourite book has remained *A Christmas Carol*. Dickens had once lived nearby on Doughty Street, where he wrote *The Pickwick Papers*, *Oliver Twist* and *Nicholas Nickleby*. It is believed that in a small courtyard in Clerkenwell he saw the pickpocket who inspired the Artful Dodger, and that on a nearby street, Oliver Twist was led to Fagin's lair. Sometimes, out for a walk, I

SUCH AN ODD WORD TO USE

imagined Dodger scudding at a rapid pace, directing Oliver to follow close at his heels.

Months earlier, while viewing properties in the area, nothing truly held my interest until I chanced upon this peculiar, detached building, set well back from the street and almost entirely veiled in wall-climbing plants. The building had begun life as a place of work before its unassuming transformation into a private home – though vestiges of its former purpose remained: thickened walls, distinctive acoustics, and tall windows set at peculiar heights. The interior was compact yet airy, and it opened onto a modest, unscreened decked terrace that overlooked the secluded garden below.

Back then, it had seemed like a modest find with hidden potential – tucked behind the terraced row, once a recording studio, and still bearing the imprint of its former life. Now, standing in that inner garden, I could almost feel the bass notes of a bygone era reverberating through soil and stone.

Then that faint thrill turned to puzzlement. There it was, lying on the doorstep – like a fragile chick pushed from its nest. The light bulb had been removed from its mounting and placed face down on the tiles. There was no note. The door was within a private space, hidden from the street. As far as I knew, no children lived nearby who might be prone to the odd playful prank. Uncertain why it was there, or by whose hand, I set it back where it belonged.

A day or two later, returning from a milk run, I found the bulb back on the doorstep. Only this time, the wall-mounted fitting was pulled loose, too. It now hung in a sorry state, straining at exposed wiring – almost as if the nest itself were clinging stubbornly to its branch, unwilling to let go.

Having recently moved to Clerkenwell, I didn't know any of the neighbours and felt reluctant to knock on door after door to see if anyone could shed light on the banished bulb.

During a workout that same week at the now long-since-closed gym, I recall recounting the unexplained events to my personal trainer, Amelia. We began with a warm-up run on a treadmill, demanding more than enough exertion to forsake any idea of talking. Then between sets of this and that, we chatted about such things as her efforts to find a good school for her kids and my settling into a new house and area. Her Scouser humour in response to the leaping light bulb story somehow made nonsense sound sensible: 'Maybe the scally got bored, trashed its home, and legged it,' she said with a mischievous grin, as if the bulb were one more fed-up tenant. And with that, she'd dispelled any residual thoughts on the mystifying occurrence.

Some days later, there was a knock at my door. Standing before me was a gentleman – perhaps in his late forties or early fifties. Polite and well-spoken, he carried the unmistakable presence of someone accustomed to leading others, his voice marked by that gentle, musical lilt you sometimes hear

SUCH AN ODD WORD TO USE

west of the Severn. A thick, lightly greying moustache framed his face, drawing attention away from his short, stocky stature and the slightly pugilistic set of his nose – flattened, perhaps, by youth or temperament. In his hand, he held the smouldering, aromatic bowl of a pipe carved from rich, dark wood – a relic of a forgotten era. It was the kind of pipe one might associate with deep thought and intricate puzzles – rare and somewhat affected for the time. He introduced himself as Alistair from the garden flat opposite, and explained with measured precision, that he had been disturbed at night by the flickering light – his bedroom window being one of many that framed the garden beyond.

My house is open-plan and unusually bright, lit by an assortment of strangely shaped windows and rooflights that seem less designed than arranged as if dictated by some forgotten acoustic logic. Yet curiously, there are no windows facing the front at all, and those upstairs are scattered high in the sloping roof in irregular positions, as if daylight were something to be filtered rather than welcomed. I therefore see my porch and the wooded garden only in the passing moments I'm coming or going. So, I was utterly unaware that on blustery days the slender branches of a newly purchased potted eucalyptus would sway and shimmer, which in turn excited the motion sensor of the outside light.

I asked why he hadn't simply knocked on my door at the outset – and whether he had pulled the mounting from the wall. His reply was short, almost curt: 'I wouldn't do that.'

A fleeting expression of pique crossed his face before softening into something resembling nostalgia, his gaze drifting to the blank porch wall – perhaps where a sign once hung. 'This used to be a music studio, you know,' he said. 'A constant to and fro of long hair and electric guitars.' He smiled faintly, then turned and walked away without another word.

Later, I found myself regretting the clumsiness of that second question, directed at a neighbour I was meeting for the first time. It would have been far better, I thought, to have simply made a casual observation. Clearly, I'd touched a nerve. But who else would have done that, if not the person disturbed?

Replacing the wall light with low footlights – the narrow, spike-in-the-ground kind often used to mark out garden paths – I arranged them in a gentle arc near the wooden porch step. Responsive to fading light rather than motion, they gave off a warm, unobtrusive glow at dusk – like a row of lit drumsticks idly waiting to be picked up.

I thought little more of it at the time. Yet in hindsight, that small incident of seemingly no consequence at all was a first splinter of kindling. The slow burn that followed would smoulder into something quietly suffocating.

Chapter 2

A Clean Cut

A few weeks passed. I worked mainly from home. I was leading an international project for a mid-sized publishing group, overseeing the roll-out of a global literary series across multiple territories. Dozens of editorial workshops had to be scheduled across several time zones, rights agreements brokered, and translation timelines brought gently into alignment. The goal was to ensure every regional imprint received a slate of titles that was neither too dense nor too lean – balanced, relevant, and locally resonant. It was a delicate kind of work: equal parts diplomacy, bureaucracy, and intuition. Gently demanding, but oddly satisfying.

Over the years, my travels have been extensive. I lived in Carravelle during an earthquake that left several high-rises cracked open like fruit, and in Darmesh at the time of a long-awaited peace accord. I spent time in Seravita, Campural, and Bridgely. Assignments in Jacuriba included trips to the old street circuits, winter carnivals, and even a river island once inhabited only by birds. For several years, weekdays working in Montvrière, Zeetrecht, and Egeborg meant flying out early on a Monday and returning late on a Friday. By the time I'd done household chores and visited family, it was time to repack and go again.

Those were exciting times, but my travelling days were largely behind me. The familiar comforts of life at home welcomed me like a returning explorer and cartographer of a distant century. Years of solitary travel and unaccompanied evening dinners made me both resilient to, and increasingly content with, a life of fewer interactions.

A small downstairs study with pocket doors was now my less-exotic destination of choice. There were no windows at eye level to distract me. Instead, the study had a recessed ceiling window that filled the room with light. I sat in a high-backed armchair of indeterminate origin, its curved wings and deep seat somehow both upright and yielding, as though designed for long hours of thought, the kind that creeps up on you unnoticed. Now and again, to stretch my neck and rest my eyes, I would tilt back my head and stare at the distant clouds floating silently overhead. Or contemplate a solitary stray oak leaf clinging to the rain-soaked walk-on glass.

A single oversized pawn stood on the narrow shelf beside the desk – beautifully carved and slightly worn, as if waiting for a chess game that might never begin. Thick, grainy, solid-wood shelves opposite me bore small clusters of hardback books, some upright, others stacked on their sides: novels, essays, travelogues, and contemplative works of philosophy. I

SUCH AN ODD WORD TO USE

loved reading about the classical and quantum realms in layman's terms, in a vain attempt to grasp the hidden hand of nature. On the desk, beside a squat potted plant with curling leaves and a small, framed family photo, sat a sleek black spider phone – then popular in smart office conference rooms.

Warmed by a bowl of porridge, and with a latte brewed from freshly ground beans close at hand, I leaned forward and tapped a button one morning for my first dial-in call of the day.

The phone line was as 'dead as a doornail', as Scrooge might have said. So, I called out an engineer. After a brief investigation, he located a break in the service cable running along the inside of the reclaimed brick wall that skirted the garden – stretching from the side access of the main building to the boundary of my house. The damage lay barely beyond my side, partly concealed in the shadows cast by tall shrubbery overhanging from the pavement.

After joining the two severed parts within a plastic housing, the engineer straightened up and frowned. It wasn't wear and tear, he said – the cable had been cleanly cut. That wasn't typical. Normally, he explained, you'd see fraying, moisture damage, or gnaw marks. Not this.

He left shortly afterwards, still frowning, and I was left standing beside the fresh repair with the strange feeling that something benign had failed to arrive on cue.

True to the principle of Occam's razor, my first thought was that the simplest – and likely innocent – explanation was the most probable.

A narrow side path – its entrance marked by a weathered, wood-slatted gate in keeping with the age of the property – ran from the street to the communal garden, skirting the length of the high secondary wall that enclosed the space. The severed cable had been clipped at a reachable height – an easy stretch for anyone passing along that path.

Perhaps, I thought, it had been a delivery gone wrong – someone wrestling a bulky item along the narrow access path, unaware that the edge of a cardboard box or steel trolley had snagged the cable and pulled it loose. Or maybe a well-meaning neighbour had taken it upon themselves to clear a patch of overgrowth, misjudging the arc of a strimmer or the reach of a long-handled tool. I even wondered whether a storm had sent a wind-snapped branch slamming against the brickwork. A fox could have made a frantic leap. A child might have chased a ball. The garden had its share of small dramas.

None of these possibilities seemed especially compelling, but all more likely, I hoped, than deliberate tampering.

But the break, the engineer had said, was clean. Not frayed. Not torn. Not weathered. Clipped. Which made the explanations feel increasingly baroque, each requiring a stranger chain of events than the last. A makeshift broom rescue gone surgical? A squirrel with wire-cutting precision? The more I replayed it, the further my thoughts drifted – not yet towards accusation, but away from accident.

I stood a while longer in the garden, turning the possibilities over in my mind, when a woman passed through, gently

SUCH AN ODD WORD TO USE

manoeuvring a pram across the uneven stone path. Her movements were careful, almost choreographed, as if she knew precisely where the bumps were hidden. She gave me a quick, tired smile – one I returned with neighbourly awkwardness – and then continued towards the far gate. I thought little of it at the time, but I sometimes wonder now if that was Lana – scarcely a few months old – tucked beneath the pram's canopy, already charting the garden's shadows in her sleep. I remember the faint clink of something hanging from the pram's handle, and the hush that followed her exit.

I wouldn't connect that moment to Lana until much later. But something about her mother's easy familiarity with the path stayed with me.

The lingering mystery of the severed cable remained undiagnosed. Perhaps a second splinter of kindling, or perhaps nothing at all. Years later, a second break occurred along the same wall. My old music studio bore these tender repairs like two carefully dressed wounds.

Chapter 3

The Number That Lied

I was happy in my new home.

It has plenty of character. The double-height vaulted ceiling gives the reception room a sense of space, light, and intimacy. A chandelier of translucent, sculpted glass hangs high above, casting soft, refracted patterns that dance across the polished concrete floor, which is sealed in a light-reflecting epoxy. Despite its modest footprint, the house feels both open and unassumingly grand. A curving staircase – its balustrade carved from pale wood, its treads lined in slate-blue felt – spirals gently to an upstairs level that wraps in an L-shape along two walls, forming a balconied platform with views across the reception below and out to the flat roof beyond.

My décor leans towards the understated, but not austere. I dislike clutter, and if something is unused, I part with it. I prefer the feeling of room to breathe, over the impulse to

SUCH AN ODD WORD TO USE

contain and store. But I wouldn't call it minimalist – that conjures images of white-on-white interiors drained of warmth or memory. I like tone and texture, but softly so.

In one corner stands an industrial display trolley – powder-coated metal, burnished with age, its castors locked slightly off-kilter. Its contents reflect my eclectic tastes. On the top shelf sits a compact bean-to-cup coffee machine beside a vintage stage microphone – chrome-grilled and heavy, mounted on a weighted base, as if waiting to be used. Below that, a neat stack of modern hardbacks is paired with a scuffed guitar pedalboard from a defunct rock band – its knobs still faintly labelled in fading marker. The bottom shelf holds three miniature chessboards, each mid-game, the pieces arranged to mirror decisive moments from classic matches: Fischer–Spassky, Kasparov–Topalov, Polgár–Karpov. To the untrained eye, they might seem like the careless scatterings of a cleaner. But to anyone who knows the game, each arrangement marks the exact moment the balance tips – victory or defeat poised on a single, silent square.

The double-height reception room offers space to indulge in art. One signed abstract I painted myself many years ago. A second purchased canvas depicts a solitary figure in profile – loosely rendered in bold acrylics, her jaw set, eyes shadowed, hair caught mid-motion as if stirred by an unseen current. It is a self-portrait, painted by a former girlfriend who studied at Central St Martins. She casts a prophetic, watchful gaze across the room, as though weighing what has passed and what is yet to come. A third fools guests. On one occasion, a visitor remarked, 'You painted this?' when looking at the abstract, then marched over to the third and said, 'This too?' – only to be embarrassed when I told them it was actually my TV displaying a Van Gogh. It looks convincingly realistic: flush to the wall, thinly framed, and displaying textures with such authenticity you could almost feel the contours of the thick, gooey oil paint.

Despite the weekday street traffic, my home feels like a peaceful sanctuary, tucked away and shielded from the noise. From the street, you'd never know it's there. I cherish this sense of seclusion, balanced by the convenience of coffee shops, restaurants, and other amenities mere moments away.

In those early weeks, the almost unnatural, though welcome, calm reignited my urge to investigate its past. When time allowed, I delved into specialised music archives, official artist biographies, and studio records, searching for the names that recorded here. To my astonishment, some major rock bands – Zinc Void, Deep Mauve, Lead Balloon, Blind Bobcat – had left their bass echoes resonating within these very walls, though I had no inkling then that those echoes ran deeper than mere metaphor. Perhaps inspired by Alistair's wistful reflection, I pictured a smoke-filled, vaulted room crammed with long hair and electric guitars. Creative harmony colliding with professional discord, as rock and vinyl spewed forth to the rapture of millions.

My house, though, bore a weirdly misleading number. By some quirk, it was known as *Studio B* – despite there being no

SUCH AN ODD WORD TO USE

A. It sat so far back from the main road that it lay physically closer to the adjoining side street, and was numbered accordingly, as if it were the first property along that street. Perhaps, before its conversion from working studio to private dwelling, there was once a direct entrance from that side – long since bricked up or reabsorbed into the surrounding wall.

The point I wish to make is that the front door was only reachable via a path linked to an address not officially recognised by Royal Mail. This invariably confused the postman. As online delivery services became the norm, parcels, post – even the occasional takeaway – often went astray, sometimes turning up days later, looking slightly apologetic.

Submitting an application to the local council, I requested both a new number and a more evocative name. I considered *Fagin's Lair*, but chose *Vinyl Vault* – a nod to its rock-recording past and the embrace of its arched ceiling.

Most Thursday afternoons, I worked from a nearby coffee shop, leaving the place to Marta, the cleaner who arrived at midday each week with a warm smile and a faded canvas tote printed with the outline of the Azores, and the long-limbed elegance of someone always slightly outpacing the world, still shaped by the loose momentum of her late twenties. She'd often begin by sharing a recent photo on her phone – a crayon masterpiece by her daughter, or the puppy curled like a comma beneath the table – describing the moment with quiet pride before I headed out and left her to it. We didn't chat for long, but there was an easy familiarity between us. She quickly intuited the rhythms of the house. The books were never to be re-shelved, the chessboards left untouched, and the bean-to-cup machine wiped with the care of a museum artefact. I liked returning to the faint scent of lavender polish and the small comfort of floors tended to with invisible care while I wasn't looking.

A few weeks in, I finally met one of the upstairs owners – Imogen, a freelance archivist who dropped by for a brief visit to her flat. She spent most of her time away, she said, letting the place out, but returned briefly to check on things and collect a few books. We spoke in the garden, where she paused to admire the fig tree. I mentioned the bizarre incidents with the cable and flickering light – she wasn't surprised. 'It's a house with layers,' she said, 'and a numbering system no sane person would have devised.' We traded a few stories and agreed it was all part of the charm. As we parted, I noticed one of the books tucked under her arm – a well-thumbed chess strategy guide. 'You play?' I asked. She smiled. 'Badly, but often.' We left it at: we should play sometime.

While working from home, I typically left the house three times a day. I'd go out for lunch, a quick afternoon stretch of the legs, and an evening run along Regent's Canal, a gym visit, or an occasional early-evening dinner at a local eatery. I recall returning home beneath a sky that seemed to be

SUCH AN ODD WORD TO USE

wringing itself out – and passing Alistair in the hallway. He made a point of welcoming me to my 'new address'. It was almost as though I'd had the entire building moved overnight. It struck me as odd, especially since I'd mentioned the application to no one. Nor was I even aware it was approved at that point. When I asked how he knew, he said plainly, 'I get alerts from the council.'

On reflection, subscribing to such alerts wasn't all that unusual. Even so, though the alerts likely related to any nearby property, I couldn't shake the slightly eerie feeling that my actions were being discreetly monitored. And it seemed as though he wanted me to know this.

A few days later, formal confirmation of my newly minted house number arrived, officially designating me a resident of *Vinyl Vault*. My home truly rocked now, and the reverberations seemed to echo everywhere. Signing up to something online, I would enter my postcode and be asked to select my address from a drop-down list – and there it was, headlining in a monotonic list of numbers and letters: *Vinyl Vault*.

In the months that followed, as life settled into its familiar rhythms, I found myself becoming increasingly wary of casual interactions with Alistair. According to one neighbour – who, with the kindest of intentions, passed along snippets about residents' backgrounds and comings and goings – his primary residence was somewhere out in the countryside – exactly where remained unclear, as if the specifics had been gently mislaid. The flat opposite served merely as a pied-à-terre. My encounters with Alistair, though infrequent, were outwardly cordial. Yet unlike the lighter, passing exchanges I enjoyed with others, conversations with him rarely stayed on the surface. It was as though certain questions were readied in advance, waiting for the right moment to be deployed. His curiosity strayed into particulars that felt uncomfortably pointed, while nothing of substance was ever offered in return.

On one occasion, as I passed by with a 'hi' that stretched the Doppler effect, Alistair drew me into a disarming and gently diverting exchange which, on reflection, revealed surprisingly little. Then, just as I made to leave, he asked for my email address – even though I lived well within range of an unraised voice. Although I have no recollection of him ever using that particular address, a replacement years later was included in group threads on the nocturnal shrieks of a resident fox, forgotten watering cans, and the mysterious reappearance of a gnome nobody claimed to own. Still, the request had felt pointed at the time – and in light of later events, I sometimes wondered whether my early wariness had been misplaced, or not misplaced enough.

And yet, there was a weight to his interest I didn't feel with anyone else.

Chapter 4

A Curious Presence

The street I lived on pulsed with weekday life – a low, habitual murmur of engines, footsteps, and shifting routines. The many leasehold flats supplied a steady flow of dog walkers, grocery shoppers, and casual joggers heading out, returning, or passing through.

In more recent years, with the advent of the homestay market, I began to run into one or two short-stay travellers wheeling their suitcase. I recall on one such occasion finding a young woman in quiet befuddlement wandering up and down the street. She was combing the façades for the home she'd booked for a couple of nights. Primed with the street name, but no number, she asked if I was local and could assist her. She showed me photos of the property, and although the briefly bashful house number had fled the scene of the shoot, I did recognise its singular frontage and was happily able to help her find her lodging.

One quickly absorbs the local rhythms – what passes for normal, and the curious variations that settle into their own uneasy harmony. And it was true even for what I might term the 'abnormal-normal' – that is to say, people who exhibit atypical behaviour relative to others but are nonetheless consistent in their own behaviour.

As a case in point, on an even busier nearby street bristling with shops and places to eat, there was a particular woman I saw quite often, over many years, heading in one direction or the other. At random intervals, she paused her walk, stood facing a shop window, or perhaps a barber shop full of bemused clientele, and performed an outrageous aerobic exercise as if in a gym class facing a wall-to-wall mirror. Or she crossed the road performing an exaggerated dance move – sometimes even stopping to face a slowing car and bewildered driver. She moved through a world of her own invention – limbs flailing with conviction, as though obeying music no one else could hear. Harmless, yes. Familiar even. The city has room for such ghosts.

Another example was an older man who routinely strolled down the same street with a pair of vibrant blue parrots – perhaps macaws – one perched on each shoulder. These dazzling shoulder pads – vaguely reminiscent of the eighties – remained unbothered by the street's clamour, drawing plenty of attention. You could easily distinguish locals from non-locals by their reactions – or lack thereof – as they passed by.

SUCH AN ODD WORD TO USE

But then came a different kind of presence – figures whose outward normality concealed something oddly scripted. Their timing, their stillness, their intent gaze – it all seemed rehearsed. That these unfamiliar figures loitered outside my home, and nowhere else, made their presence particularly unsettling.

I'd like to paint the picture of one or two such figures.

Traipsing home one time, after popping out for a few essentials, I noticed a shabbily dressed man who looked, at first glance, to be homeless, standing on the pavement. He faced the black railings in front of the building behind which my house resided. It could almost have been Fagin himself back on one of his favoured streets. At his side was a rickety lightweight shopping trolley, seemingly holding all his worldly possessions. Dressed in a dishevelled hat and a muted, distressed scarf, he bowed his head while tapping intently on a smartphone.

There was something dissonant in his dexterous use of the device and the gracefulness of his movements. His frame and posture conveyed a peak of fitness. And his deliberate positioning pressed up against the wrought-iron railings, like a jailed man, also felt strange. It was almost as if any further inch between him and the building was of real consequence. All were at odds with the persona it seemed he wished to project.

On another occasion, I returned home to find a young woman I'd never seen before, inside the property's boundary.

Casually dressed in jeans and white trainers, she perched on one of the three stone steps leading up to the racing green door. There were no bags to suggest a respite from shopping. There was no suitcase to suggest a mistaken address. Legs splayed, she sat hunched over, and intensely focused on, a small device. She seemed oblivious to my presence, or at least wanted to convey that impression. When I asked who she was waiting for, she merely shrugged and left without uttering a word.

Perhaps a year later, I saw what appeared to be the same woman, once again seated on the steps and staring at her phone. This time, I was on my way out. As I passed, she abruptly put the phone to her ear and bellowed, 'Hello,' as if projecting to the back row of a West End theatre. At the same time, she craned her head towards me with what felt like a warning glare, as if to say, *Don't even think about engaging with me this time.* I couldn't avoid the distinct feeling that there was no one on the other end.

From time to time, a 4x4 would park strangely, perched needlessly on the pavement by the railings. Always the same spot in front of my address. The driver would remain inside, manipulating a small device. I'd notice them when popping out to the shop – and often, they'd still be there when I returned. It was not the kind of vehicle used by a ride-hailing service, and this was anyway a time dominated almost exclusively by London's traditional and distinctive black cabs. On one occasion I saw the car both arrive and, after a short period

SUCH AN ODD WORD TO USE

of device fiddling, depart – the driver did not drop off, pick up or leave the vehicle.

There were others, too – barely glimpsed, easily forgotten, yet strangely persistent.

And, since the front of the main building isn't visible from my house, I could only assume that the instances I did notice, in those usually brief moments of coming or going, were but a small sample of all the shadowy visitors. I never observed such furtive behaviour outside any of the surrounding properties.

Who were these curious figures, folded neatly into the margins of my days – each clutching a device, each momentarily cast in a role I hadn't written? And what scene, I wondered, were we playing out?

Chapter 5

The Home That Wasn't

One summer, hoping to make fuller use of the roof terrace overlooking the garden, I emailed the local council's planning department. I wanted to know whether I could install a railing around the terrace without needing to submit a full planning application.

An important feature of this process was its confidentiality – unless a related application was eventually filed, the enquiry would remain private. I already felt under remote observation, like a buoy bobbing on still water, its every shift monitored for the faintest ripple. I simply wanted to test the waters without causing waves.

Planning replied that a railing would indeed require a formal application. Intriguingly, they added that I could apply for a certificate confirming the lawfulness of the existing decked area – provided I could prove it had been in place for over four years, which by now it had.

SUCH AN ODD WORD TO USE

♪

By the new year, having acted on neither part of the council's advice, I decided to put my house on the market. I had lived at *Vinyl Vault* longer than anywhere else I'd called home. I was open to a change of scene and increasingly unsettled by the strange characters who seemed to gravitate towards the property, like actors drawn to an audition.

On idle weekends, I wandered through Wimbledon Village. I hadn't planned on moving to that side of town, but something about its atmosphere – bookshops, broad greens, and unhurried ease – lodged itself in my mind.

The sales agent I chose did a splendid job. They were able to get a full-page ad in several magazines and, best of all, a feature in the property section of a national broadsheet. The spread included a dramatic strapline inspired by a recently released movie, aimed squarely at young bankers in London's Square Mile.

The eponymous *The Big Short* reference felt like a bit of a stretch for such a modest house, but it made me smile, and I admired their ambition – playing, as it did, to London's financially literate and cynically inclined. It worked, too – the marketing generated strong interest and led to a series of promising viewings in a buoyant housing market. I didn't spot the irony at the time – the nod to a shortable asset would soon strike uncomfortably close to home.

Then came the call. The estate agent's sales director said Alistair, my neighbour across the garden, had contacted the office more than once to dispute the listing's reference to the terrace as amenity space.

Alistair's intervention pushed me to revisit the idea of formalising lawful use. A search of the planning portal led me to a consultant who had secured success for a similar roof terrace nearby. I reached out for advice, as there was now every likelihood of an objection.

Then, something odd happened.

I had discussed the matter with no one but the consultant – no decision made, no forms submitted. Still, one afternoon, I heard Alistair's voice through an open window as I wandered past. He was mid-call, his tone edged with tension, the phrase '... an underhand planning application...' carrying just enough to catch in my ear like a sleeve on bramble. I kept walking, feigning disinterest – but the words stayed with me.

Then, from across the hush of the garden, a small voice called out.

'Do you live in that little house?'

I looked up to see a young girl – six or seven, perhaps – perched near the base of the central tree. Her plaits were uneven, her leggings a mismatch of patterns, and her expression carried the grave confidence of someone used to asking questions and expecting answers.

'I'm Lana,' she added, before I could respond. 'I live up there.' She pointed to one of the upper flats with a gap-toothed grin. Raised solely by her English mother, Lana spoke in the careful, vowel-smooth accent of the Islington prep-school set – no trace of her American father remained, at least not in her voice. 'I'm six and three-quarters,' she added, with the precise authority only small children seem to possess. 'Mummy says the lights at night look like fairy circles. Did you know?'

'No,' I said, 'but I'll keep an eye out.'

She nodded. 'You should also know there's a fox with one eye and a bird that steals biscuits.'

Then she vanished behind a planter as swiftly as she'd appeared.

And for a moment, I forgot all about Alistair's words.

A week later, I stepped outside again. The garden held its usual hush – that muffled stillness you sometimes get in a small, half-forgotten woodland. Lana – her hair pulled back in two uneven pigtails – was skipping between patches of moss and bark mulch, the rope making a soft whuff each time it brushed the earth.

'Hi, Lana,' I said.

She stopped skipping at once, fixed me with a serious look, and planted her hands on her hips.

'Are you building a roof garden?' she asked, as if accusing me of hiding sweets.

I blinked. 'Pardon?'

She nodded, solemnly. 'The man with the smoky pipe told my mummy you're building one.'

For a moment, I was caught off guard. I'd told no one. No forms had been submitted. I'd barely made up my own mind. And yet here it was, a skipping child in a sun-faded jumper giving form to those enigmatic words I'd overheard the prior week.

Trying to smile, I asked, 'Do you think I should?'

She considered it. 'Yes. But not with pokey plants. They ruin everything. You need soft things. And maybe a beanbag.'

Then she resumed skipping, losing herself again in the soft rhythms of the garden.

I watched her go – each hop and swing precisely measured, as if she were following some secret beat only she could hear. A few days earlier, I'd noticed her crouched on the steps with a little notebook, tongue poking out slightly, scribbling in a large looping hand. 'It helps me un-jumble things,' she'd said when she saw me looking. 'When I don't know what something means, I write it down and draw pictures till it stops being all wiggly in my head.'

That image lingered. A skipping rope, a pencil, and a resolute insistence on clarity – tools more powerful than they looked.

I stood there for a while longer, the rope's soft rhythm still brushing the edge of thought, and wondered how Alistair could possibly know.

SUCH AN ODD WORD TO USE

♪

Back indoors, my to-and-fro with the consultant took a sharp turn for the worse. His research had uncovered an issue that rocked the house and shook me along with it: my former recording studio – the entire house – was never formally recognised as residential. Although it was renovated as a home, it was still officially classed as a place of work. How on earth had my solicitor missed that? Was I now living in a worthless pile of bricks?

For a moment, I was back in my tenth-floor apartment in Carravelle, before the turn of the millennium, woken by a shaking bed, thrashing clothes hangers, cracks appearing in the walls, and a TV cabinet rolling across the room, straining at its cable. Nearby, roads buckled and older buildings fell. Were my present-day walls crumbling around me?

It marked the beginning of several very stressful months. But there was more than one thread of hope: if I could prove I'd lived in the property for more than four years – which I had – then changing its planning classification should be possible. And with that, approval for the roof terrace would likely follow. Even so, the situation remained precarious.

Without the correct residential designation, I now had no choice but to take my property off the market and pursue a path to fix the issue. It was frustrating to lose all that marketing exposure that would be so difficult to repeat. But in hindsight, any sale would likely have fallen through once the lack of authorised residential use inevitably came to light.

♪

I began to notice small things. A glance held a little too long from a window across the garden. A polite but unusually pointed question from another neighbour about roof access. It was subtle – nothing I could quite pin down – but the sense grew that word had spread.

And not by accident.

My consultant prepared the paperwork, and for the avoidance of doubt, made it explicitly clear that it included official recognition of the terrace. This was sent off to Planning. And thus began a formal eight-week process.

At least one objection was firmly expected. What I had not foreseen was an orchestrated call-to-arms. And one, I realised, I unwittingly helped fuel.

Chapter 6

A Letter Too Far

To clear out some unwanted items, I booked a 'too big for the bin' waste collection with the council. Without a car, and preferring to walk wherever possible, I relied on these occasional pickups for anything unwieldy. I had space left in my quota, so I asked a neighbour if they had anything to add. It also served as a polite heads-up that bulky items would be outside for a few hours on the appointed day.

That weekend, a note arrived – folded into thirds inside a pale blue envelope, the kind you might associate with a birthday card. It was unsigned, written in looping, slanted handwriting with careful spacing and occasional flourishes. A quiet thank you for 'offering to include additional items in your collection' was followed by a second, more arresting line: 'a letter is being circulated encouraging residents to object to your planning application.' Attached, by a square of tape, was a photocopy of that very letter.

The timing made me pause. I had arranged the collection in good faith – and now someone had used the moment to press this into my hand *in absentia*. But the tone lingered: measured, precise, and somehow sympathetic. It felt less like a warning and more like a discreet gesture of solidarity. As though the sender disagreed with what was being done but preferred to stay unnamed. No return address. Just the faint trace of lavender – and the sense that someone, somewhere, was on my side.

The letter itself struck an alarmist tone, casting a wide net. Anonymous, yet assertive, it urged neighbours to object swiftly, warning darkly of unbridled festivities and barbecue smoke clouds of unprecedented density. The language had the flavour of a melodrama: *Act I. Scene 1. A peaceful neighbourhood under siege.*

In moments of rising anxiety like these, I try to make light of them – exaggerating to the point of absurdity. I recall visualising hostile billboards, multilingual leaflet drops, and TV spots featuring banner-waving, placard-carrying crowds. It helped me regain a sense of proportion.

And yet, the tightly packed panes of neighbouring glass enclosing the garden on all sides suggested an already over-the-top response. Walls of windows faced one another like battalions amassed on either side of a nineteenth-century battlefield. Balconies – like watchtowers – flanked me to the

SUCH AN ODD WORD TO USE

right, and a roof terrace to the left. The letter felt excessive – as though it were rooted in something deeper.

In the end, many let the call-to-arms drift past like one of the high clouds above my rooflight. Only two neighbours formally objected. Names and comments redacted. The faint trace of opposition – recorded, but faceless.

Chapter 7

Behind the Ironed Curtain

It was hard not to wonder what might lie behind those well-drawn curtains.

It felt like more than coincidence that Alistair's latest stay dovetailed so precisely with the application process. I imagined the game was afoot, and this was merely the next act in a longer drama. I pictured his rural retreat left in anticipatory stillness – a vacated war room with curtains half-drawn, a low lamp still burning, and the faint aroma of oak-cured pipe tobacco curling through the air – less a lingering scent than a memory of someone recently departed.

For weeks, the bedroom windows across the dappled garden from my decked space were permanently flung open – the twin bores of Napoleonic field guns trained skyward, poised to repel any rooftop incursion. Humour would be my shield during these uncertain weeks.

SUCH AN ODD WORD TO USE

Knowing it was standard practice during the planning process for a case officer to visit the property, I couldn't help but wonder what Machiavellian tactic Alistair might devise. Would he don his pyjamas, sweep aside the net curtains, and stage a dramatic performance directed at the intrusive presence – the unwitting emissary?

As it happened, the request for advice, made a year earlier, came to my assistance. By sheer luck, the same aptly named officer, Hannah Bricks, was assigned to my current case. Since she had already visited the terrace, a second visit was not necessary.

My reference to a 'next act' wasn't simply acknowledging the call-to-arms – I felt certain Alistair had already laid some groundwork.

Shortly after I had received a response to my confidential planning query the previous summer, Alistair replaced his bedroom window. It wasn't part of any wider refurbishment – just the one, freed of external security bars and recast with side-hung casements dressed in a polite Georgian pastiche – tall, slender panes framed like a modest fringe-theatre stage, newly eager for West End attention. The final audience member – the planning officer – need only slip in and take in the understated production, its scenery so carefully set.

I considered saying something – some brief but direct inquiry that might pierce the veil. But I held back. It felt too early, too revealing. There was a chance, still, that the application might proceed without incident, and I saw no reason to hand him any further advantage. Besides, part of me suspected that confrontation was exactly what he wanted – that the staging, the faintly theatrical provocations, were designed to draw me in. Better, I thought, to stay out of reach. To observe, record, and trust that the process – though never perfect – might yet lean in my favour.

The eight-week process though ended in muted defeat. The threads of hope I clung to began to unravel.

Chapter 8

A Spooked Withdrawal

Hannah Bricks from Planning rang me directly with the bad news – they couldn't grant the application. There was a pause, just long enough to make me wonder if she was choosing her words, before she said they'd been 'spooked' by the objections. The way she said it – light, almost ironic – left me unsure whether she meant the objections themselves, or the objector. Either way, it was such an odd word to use.

The stress of living in my non-home was wearing me down. I thought wistfully of the day I bought my very first flat. My second, third and fourth followed – each a rung on that ever-quickening ladder. The story of those four was so uneventful by comparison. And now, on the fifth, had I stepped onto a rung that splintered beneath me?

Fortunately, all hope was not entirely lost. The advice of the case officer was to withdraw the current application and submit a new one. This time, it needed to include a formal statutory declaration to remove any doubt about my residential use of the property for more than four years. I understood the council's position. With Alistair kicking up quite a fuss, they had no choice but to dot every 'i' and cross every 't'.

The declaration required me to solemnly and sincerely affirm several points, with a couple of dozen pages of exhibits – an exhausting effort given the one-sided transparency. The objectors remained unnamed – their comments, redacted. Meanwhile, I had to disclose a swathe of sensitive documents, including personal letters from my cleaner and trainer confirming four years' residence. Marta's was handwritten with contact details in her precise, slightly floral script, folded with care and delivered one Thursday afternoon alongside the usual post-clean note. All this private information remained online for years, a fact I discovered only recently and promptly moved to correct.

One morning, a letter arrived addressed simply to 'The Occupier'. Inside was a flyer for a private security firm – printed on glossy card, with a photograph of a smartly dressed guard standing beside an iron gate. *Discreet. Vigilant. Experienced in sensitive planning matters.* No price. No sender address. Merely a telephone number and a motto: *Guardians of Outlook and Amenity.* I threw it in the bin. Then fished it out again. An hour later, I binned it for good.

SUCH AN ODD WORD TO USE

With the papers signed and witnessed by a law firm, the clock restarted on another eight-week process. Emboldened objectors now had even more time to weigh in.

Adding to my chagrin, Planning also refused my consultant's request to see the actual objection letters. Instead, they shared only a couple of brief quotes alongside their official responses. Whatever 'spooked' them left only the faintest footprint.

Chapter 9

When the Curtain Falls

I don't think I ever took so many anxious walks. As the process dragged on, I'd pace along streets, head bowed, oblivious to everything around me. My mind churned over the possible motives behind what felt like such intense opposition. I worried over what fresh attempts might be made to scupper my new application. At times, I physically shook at the thought of the potential consequences for my home.

Amid the slow grind of planning bureaucracy, my work carried on. I spent hours each week in remote editorial workshops – my screen dividing me from colleagues in Delhi, São Paulo, Toronto. Time zones blurred, and coffee became both ritual and necessity. There were rights agreements to finesse, translation schedules to untangle, and subtle cultural tensions to balance – delicate work, part diplomacy, part logistics. Each regional imprint had its own

SUCH AN ODD WORD TO USE

preferences, constraints, and market realities, and my task was to align them without friction. It helped to anchor me. While part of my mind remained tethered to the strange theatre surrounding my home, this global project offered a different kind of intensity – challenging, yes, but in a way that gave rather than drained.

Then, after months of circling delays – spring softened into the long hush of late summer – the application was finally granted.

♪

I felt no joy, or even satisfaction. Just pure unadulterated relief.

That stretch of time now seemed dreamlike. The days unfurled one after another – bud-tipped branches giving way to soft evenings and lengthening shadows. I measured their passing not by calendars, but by the arc of light on the walls, the shifting scent of the garden, the occasional neighbour's remark. And then, almost as if it had drifted into being rather than arrived, the decision.

My thoughts turned slowly to those letters. Had it not been for that use of the word 'spooked', I'm not sure I would have pursued them. Its very mention gnawed at me – I needed to understand what lay behind it all. This did not feel run-of-the-mill in the least, especially given that my home itself had been at stake.

Poring over government legislation, I searched for any rights to obtain copies of objection letters. Though I no longer recall the precise statute or provision, I found something. A formal request followed, and the response from the council was positive. The only condition was that I had to collect them in person.

I took a long walk to the Town Hall, where a cubicle clerk finally handed me the letters I'd waited months to see. Without reading them, I headed home.

Along the way, I tried to shed the emotional residue of that overlong process. I needed to adopt a more neutral mindset – to see the objections as the system intended: a chance for neighbours to raise valid concerns about noise or privacy. What complicated things was the inseparability of the residential use of the house from the lawful use of the terrace.

The second objector wasn't entirely unexpected. He was the kind of neighbour every community values without fuss – seen jogging each morning, cheerfully asking after Lana's mum, or following up on a seafood recommendation. His interest was always sincere, his courtesy unfailing. But beneath that warmth lay a prim satisfaction in protocol, a tidy deference to procedure. Like Dickens's Mr Wemmick, he rarely missed a deadline, and his responses – always polite, well-reasoned – reminded you that rules existed for a reason.

Unlike the second objector, whose commitment to the rules carried no edge, the first objector's motives felt darker, more personal.

SUCH AN ODD WORD TO USE

His objection arrived like a flurry of strikes – distinct, deliberate, landing in a calculated rhythm. They revealed the objector's full name – a detail that would soon lead me to an explanation for that enigmatic 'spooked' comment. They would shed some light, too, on the strange visitors to the property – though not fully on what they were doing.

The first came like an uppercut – formal, procedural, but clearly designed to forestall further steps. Yet it only deepened my puzzlement over how he could be so sure an application was forthcoming. The 'man with the smoky pipe' told Lana's mum I was building a roof garden. Yet, for me, it was still only a distant possibility – something being tentatively discussed with an independent planning consultant.

Reading it prompted the return of a particular memory – one that crystallised Alistair's unease around my house. It had followed a leak in the flat roof. I stood at the side of the building, shaded by a mature sycamore tree, while two roof specialists examined the upper level from the garden below. As we discussed possible causes, Alistair suddenly appeared, arms flailing in a pantomime of alarm – as if seeking our urgent attention.

'You're not building up, are you?' he blurted.

'No, I'm trying to fix a leak,' I replied – sharper than I intended.

He hovered for a moment, but said no more. I could have asked what prompted the outburst, could have pressed him

CARL GOODWIN

on his assumptions – but I let it go. Better, I decided, not to feed the fire.

What lingered in my mind wasn't the words exchanged, but the visible strain in his face, his voice, his whole bearing. At the time, it struck me as oddly disproportionate. Building upwards required consultation and approvals – there was no cause for such immediate distress.

Perhaps that moment should have warned me – because when I returned to the letters, it was a sharp jab that struck next, followed by a sequence of combinations. Letters striking from all angles, some low, some high, each landing with calculated intent. A few were heavy with legalese and edged with aggression, others pared back to an unobstructed view from a ground-floor window – each searching for a decisive blow as the final seconds ticked away. All were signed with the same bold, inky flourish, flared with the confidence of a pair of flamboyant boxing shorts.

Later, I retrieved the anonymous call-to-arms – the one folded in thirds and slipped into the pale blue envelope. It bore the same date as Alistair Greyburn's initial objection and echoed the phrasing of his flurry of letters with unnerving precision.

I let them sit for a while, untouched – breathing in their typography and tone. What struck me first was the alignment: the same generous margins, the same faintly antique font, the same neatly indented paragraphs. The phrasing carried a peculiar cadence – a clipped rhythm that broke thoughts into tidy

SUCH AN ODD WORD TO USE

segments, as if written for the eye of an institution rather than a neighbour. Certain expressions reappeared, dressed in slightly different contexts but unmistakably cut from the same cloth.

Then there was the formality – a kind of composed vehemence that suggested experience, a comfort in officialese. These were not hastily written notes dashed off between errands. They were structured – paragraphs marshalled, phrases chosen for weight and effect. Even the signature, where present, had a certain theatrical boldness, as if asserting not merely identity but authority.

The resemblance was not simply visual, but tonal. Whether drafted directly or guided at a distance, the hand behind the rallying letter was, in all likelihood, the same that had shaped the objections. The mask had slipped – not entirely, but enough.

Out of curiosity, I searched for the name Alistair Greyburn. I expected to find a commonplace LinkedIn profile or such like. But what I found was a dated newspaper feature buried in the archives – one that described him as a former Cabinet Office adviser, 'one of those mandarins you'd never find on an org chart, but everyone knew handled the approvals no one talked about.' It gave new weight to the word 'spooked'. And new shape to the silence that followed. The inset photo confirmed what I already suspected – this was the man 'spooking' the council.

♪

As none of his letters explicitly referenced any government connections, I was left wondering how the 'spooked' comment from the council had been prompted. It seemed plausible to me that Alistair may have personally visited the Town Hall during the process. Perhaps he had referred to his background in discussions. That could have left an impression. To help ground my perspective, I imagined satellite photographs of my terrace and earnest protestations about its supposed risk to national security.

It was the relentlessness of Alistair's deliveries that left me reeling – the volume, the precision, the angles of attack. Each letter carefully pitched, formally phrased, and unmistakably forceful.

I had half a mind to laminate the letters and bind them: *Opposition: A Memoir in Endless Acts.* Perhaps there'd be a reading in a draughty church hall, Alistair centre stage beneath a dusty spotlight, declaiming each paragraph with sombre relish. Admission free. Donations to the cause.

There was something else that irked me too. None of the letters made it clear that there was no objection to the residential use of the house. His words focused on the flat roof, yes, but could he not have clarified that his concerns were confined solely to the terrace? There appeared to be no empathy with the predicament I was in.

By now, Alistair seemed aware that I'd obtained the letters, though I'd mentioned them to no one but my consultant. This became evident when I bumped into him in the communal

SUCH AN ODD WORD TO USE

garden one day. He was standing among the ivy-edged beds, pruning secateurs in hand, when he turned to me without preamble and said, 'I wrote some letters.' Then, with a slight tilt of the head, he asked, 'Would you consider screening off the terrace?'

There it was. The closest thing to an admission I would ever get. But it didn't feel like an olive branch – it felt more like an inventory check. As if he needed to confirm exactly what I knew, and whether I'd do what he wanted regardless.

The economy of his words was disappointing. Here was another chance – missed – to ease tensions, to offer some explanation or at least acknowledge the broader impact of his campaign. Instead, he presented it as an afterthought, an offhand remark tucked into a passing encounter.

Still, I replied that I did plan to screen off the terrace. Despite everything, I wasn't entirely unsympathetic. There was something strangely human about his unease – its roots tangled, perhaps, in age, memory, or control.

With the lawful use resolved, I had hoped things might settle down after that brief exchange. They did not. From then on, it felt as though I'd joined the cast of characters myself – miscast as a bad actor from some enemy state.

Chapter 10

Devices Gone Rogue

Now that I knew of Alistair's former position, I reflected again on the reasonableness of his actions. I could understand why Alistair might have grounds for occasional checks on the security of his flat.

Still, I couldn't quell the feeling that some of his actions may have ventured a little beyond the pale. That sureness of my intent to create a roof garden. The 'spooked' comment, hinting at an exertion of influence. And then those shadowy figures with their small devices. Were they scanning for anything that might pose a genuine concern? Or were they seeking devices that could be turned to monitor the private information of others? I had no evidence of this, but the mere possibility unsettled me.

SUCH AN ODD WORD TO USE

It was as though Alistair wanted me to feel his ever-watchful gaze. His kitchen stood across the bramble-skirted garden, well within the reach of a tree's shadow wandering before dusk. I recall that around this time, a small cube-shaped box appeared on an otherwise bare window sill, positioned between the glass pane and the blinds. It looked as though it had been carefully angled so that its sides faced outward at forty-five degrees to the window. Each outward-facing surface displayed a drawing of a large eye. Those eyes appeared to follow me every time I ventured out.

Over time, I began to form the impression that he kept the kitchen blinds closed while in residence – as suggested by open windows or the warm spill of evening light – but left them wide open in his absence. I wondered why he would go to the trouble of opening the blinds when leaving. Perhaps it meant nothing – simply a habit. But whether true or not, it was hard to dislodge the feeling there might be more to it – maybe even a hidden device deeper in the kitchen, adding a genuine lens to those drawn eyes.

At the time, I'd been more than a bit lax with regard to my personal digital security. With careless disregard, I'd even thrown out a spare, well-used window remote – the kind that controlled the opening and closing of high-set blinds and windows. And I did so without first disabling it. Not long after, the electric blinds opened or closed at random without any prompt from me. In all the years I had lived here, this had never happened. Not once. After a few such occurrences over several weeks, the behaviour stopped.

With a new resolve, I shored up my home and digital security in various ways. Doing so gave me some small measure of control and peace of mind. I even threw out my sleek black spider phone and abandoned use of a landline altogether. Voice communications over the Internet were by then the protocol of my employer, so a landline was no longer needed.

♪

I chanced upon a prototype product described as a 'caller ID for the front door'. This small WiFi-enabled device fitted snugly onto the inside of my optical door viewer. Whenever the door vibrated – whether from knocking, opening, or closing – it would instantly send a few seconds of live video to my phone. This allowed me to decide whether or not to answer. And it worked well.

Until it didn't.

After weeks of flawless operation, the device started to behave erratically. It would record at random, even when nothing at all was happening. And it would not stop until I manually intervened. I appeared to have no control over it. I contacted the supplier to report the strange behaviour. And I threw it out shortly afterwards.

Not long after, I came across another popular product that plugged into a home WiFi router. It notified me of any

SUCH AN ODD WORD TO USE

attempt to join my private network, allowing me to approve or block requests in real time. It also had an interesting feature that created a kind of 'digital fence' that looked for unusual devices within a given radius of the home. It had no sense of direction – merely flagged nearby signals in the same way that *Settings > WiFi* on an iOS device lists nearby networks.

The concept of a digital fence likely works well in less densely populated areas. An unexplained reading outside one's home might be helpful to know about. In a dense urban environment, the sheer number of signals all around you has the opposite effect. It would be akin to worrying about every spam email received. I soon threw that out too.

An established brand of doorbell camera now stood watch at my door. Perhaps this porch-posted sentry would offer a more secure way of monitoring any unwelcome visitors. My intention had never been to intrude – only to safeguard my home and private information, discreetly and without spectacle. It was only the strange characters, and Alistair's eerie knowledge of private details, that drove me to install such a device.

Most days, the camera captured little more than the languid choreography of the garden – rustling ivy, circling pigeons, a single empty crisp packet that appeared with such frequency I began to suspect it was on some kind of reconnaissance. Occasionally, someone would drift into frame, pause near the gate, and melt away again – another silent audition for the ever-expanding cast.

But gradually, the tone began to shift.

The doorbell camera started logging visits that felt less like accidents of footfall and more like intent – figures loitering outside my front door, hands in pockets, eyes scanning, then gone. No delivery. No knock. I had trusted the camera to offer clarity, a small shield against uncertainty. But even that, it turned out, was not as secure as I believed.

♪

That evening, I logged on for my weekly chess game with Imogen. She was away again – this time in Portugal, researching the evolution of place names – but she appeared online with her usual punctuality. Her username materialised on the screen with a familiar warble.

Imogen: 1.e4

Me: c5

Imogen: Ah. Playing it safe. Has the packet returned?

Me: It's practically a resident. I've started to wonder if it's not just a crisp packet but some kind of reconnaissance drone.

We exchanged a few more moves. She developed with deliberate restraint – knight, bishop, knight – then fianchettoed her dark-square bishop and tucked her king away behind a low, bristling line of pawns. The Hedgehog. A compact little fortress, all defence and latent menace.

SUCH AN ODD WORD TO USE

Me: Clever girl. The Hedgehog System. The moves of a passive-aggressive controlling observer.

I paused a moment, watching the pieces settle into their careful formation. It was the kind of position that looked innocuous – cautious, even – but from which a sudden shift could be launched without warning. I wondered whether she had picked it deliberately. I wondered, too, how it felt to play a system so closely aligned with how I'd been living: withdrawn, observant, hedged.

Imogen: Thought it might suit your current ... habitat.

A soft touch, that line – enough to show she was paying attention, without making a thing of it.

Me: New installation in his kitchen window. A small cube, tastefully wedged between the pane and the blinds. Each face features a large eye, hand-drawn. I assume it's decorative. Though it does seem to swivel when I step outside.

Imogen: Sounds artisanal.

Imogen: Maybe he's moonlighting as a surveillance sculptor.

She castled short. I advanced a pawn. Our conversation shifted to lighter matters – the book she'd recently finished and a derelict theatre she'd stumbled upon.

But even as we played, I couldn't quite shake the feeling that our weekly game had become more than a friendly ritual. It was a steady constant – moves on a board, messages in a window – but also a way of anchoring myself, of letting someone else bear witness to the slow drift of oddities accumulating at my door.

Chapter 11

Three Harbingers

The doorbell camera began its silent watch in mid-July, and a second took up position over the door to my roof terrace – like pawns shielding their king, unblinking sentries in a game whose rules kept changing.

Six weeks later, the first of three silent visitors, each like a spectral walk-on from a half-forgotten play – oddly reminiscent of Ebenezer Scrooge's three ghosts – materialised in the private garden.

All signs indicated Alistair was in residence: the garden-facing kitchen window stood open, blinds drawn – the bedroom windows half-ajar, their net curtains stirring faintly in the evening air.

It was a bright, warm late-summer evening when a man in white trainers, jeans, and a blue patterned short-sleeved shirt cautiously emerged from the side path. His eyes were

SUCH AN ODD WORD TO USE

fixed keenly on my doorbell, almost as if he'd been pre-briefed on its presence. In his left hand, he held a slip of paper. His right hand rested partially in his pocket, seemingly concealing something. He slowly walked out of view towards the corner of the enclosed garden. He made a show of looking around, as though marvelling at some wondrous museum exhibit long buried and newly unearthed. In reality, he was facing nothing more than reclaimed brickwork.

He remained out of shot for about forty seconds before reappearing. He positioned himself in front of my porch, a little to one side. Holding a phone in his right hand, he appeared to take two quick photos at different angles, with only the briefest pause to frame and focus. Visualising the lines passing through his eyes and phone, the trajectories pointed to two likely focal points: the doorbell and the terrace camera. Then, with studied nonchalance, he turned and sauntered back down the side path.

In all my years here, I'd never seen anyone behave like a random tourist in this hidden, private garden – tucked behind an unremarkable terrace on a wholly unremarkable street. My home's rock past was long buried and there was certainly nothing remotely photo-worthy about the doorbell or terrace camera. And even if there had been, they wouldn't have been visible to a passer-by – unless, of course, the very objective was to capture images of those two cameras, perhaps to confirm their make and model.

I replayed the two-minute video and turned up the sound. On the second playback, I noticed something I had missed the first time.

The camera captured only the entrance to the side path. Its view formed a narrow diagonal across the space – from the near-left edge of the alleyway to the opposite wall a short way in – creating a wedge-shaped frame that revealed the nearest corner. Most of the passage, including the side door to Alistair's kitchen, remained out of sight.

One minute and fifteen seconds into the recording, the partial silhouette of the mystery character – outlined from the back of the head to the heel – pauses briefly at Alistair's door, delivers a sharp double-rap that pounds like a drummer's snare, then pivots and presses his back to the wall as though instinctively avoiding the camera's gaze, a single hand flicking into view to momentarily disrupt the frame as indistinct mutterings drift through the audio – low, unintelligible – before the interaction ends and the short clip concludes, leaving an uneasy stillness.

I had never seen this man before, and I never saw him again in the years that followed. I wasn't sure what to make of it all.

It crossed my mind that, in addition to taking the two photos, he might have placed or collected something in the garden. Or perhaps he was merely scouting and photographing the best location for a later placement. The corner in question – tucked just out of view of my doorbell camera

– was partially concealed by a dense cluster of pots and shade-loving shrubs, the sort that thrived in this lightly overgrown patch. It struck me as an ideal hiding place – if that's what it was – but without knowing what I was meant to find, any search felt both speculative and futile.

Six days later, a second visitor appeared in the communal garden. Their behaviour was stranger still – and once again, there seemed to be a link with Alistair. What unfolded involved more than the camera could capture.

It was early evening – around a quarter to six – on another warm, bright day. I was heading out to grab something to eat. Alistair's windows onto the greenery were open. In the doorbell recording, the first thing visible was me exiting through the front door, crossing the garden, and disappearing into the side access.

Off-camera, I walked down the path and onto the street. As I approached the street, I noticed a man crossing the road towards me. He was wearing black padded over-ear headphones, talking, and carrying a rucksack slung over one shoulder. As I reached the pavement, he abruptly stopped and appeared to take a photo of the rather average-looking, in fact at that time I would say rather decrepit, main building. Its once-deep racing green door was peeling at the edges, exposing a patchwork of pale undercoat and bare wood, while the fluted pilasters flanking it had begun to crumble, their fragments gathering in the creases of the old stone steps. Even the sunburst fanlight above seemed dulled, its glass clouded, rimmed in dust. Yet, had we suddenly become a tourist hotspot?

As I turned left and walked down the road, I glanced back and was relieved to see the man walking away in the opposite direction. A few moments later, I crossed at the lights and headed towards the local eateries.

Later, I would watch back the recording and, during this uneventful segment from the camera's point of view, I couldn't help but picture Alistair, behind the net curtains of his front room, observing the scene. I imagined him instructing headphones-guy: 'Stop. Wait. Take a photo. Walk away,' when I emerged from the side path – clearly unscripted.

Returning to the action, barely a few steps further, my phone buzzed with an alert. My diligent little doorbell was now sending me video of the same man inside the private garden, near my front door. It was one minute and forty seconds since my recorded exit. He must have walked a few yards down the road, then doubled back. Curious, I did the same, eager to see what was happening.

Meanwhile, the camera showed the bearded man – dressed in a black biker jacket, black trousers, and black shoes – walking out of view through the wooded garden, still talking as he went. His path cut across at a sharp, deliberate, almost-obtuse angle – heading straight for the same shadowed corner where the man in the blue-patterned shirt had lingered.

Thirty seconds later, he reappeared in view of the camera, heading towards the path. He paused – still talking – his expression clouded with confusion, then turned abruptly and disappeared once more into the garden. Twenty seconds later, the corner of the bedroom net curtain drew back, and Alistair's head briefly appeared, his smiling face turned and tilted as if observing headphones-guy. Moments later, the man reappeared, walking steadily towards the side path before vanishing from view.

Golden light lingered, but the air felt faintly unsettled – as though the roles had shifted, and I had begun wandering back towards someone else's scene. Halfway along, I saw the man emerge onto the main street and head towards me. Our paths crossed, and I returned to my front door, leaving it ajar, wondering what to make of the situation.

But this little episode wasn't yet over.

Four minutes and forty seconds into the recording – only twenty seconds after my return – the man reappeared. He paused on the side path, craning his head to look directly at my now-ajar front door. Then, seemingly satisfied no one stood at the threshold, he moved off-camera once more towards the evidently magnetic cluster of pots and shrubs, before finally departing – five minutes into the recording.

The third little theatrical event was slicker – and occurred three days later. Shortly before midday, yet another unfamiliar figure emerged, entering stage left via the side path. Holding a phone screen-up in his right hand and a small flat parcel in his left, he walked confidently out of view, stage right. He remained off-camera for around fifteen seconds before reappearing, speaking into the white earbud nestled in his left ear.

What struck me first was how, the moment he entered, his gaze fixed on what was fast becoming a rather popular corner of the garden.

The second striking detail was his bulging belly – it looked false. His two-tone grey and red short-sleeved shirt hung awkwardly, with a gaping opening at the hem that seemed almost designed for quick storage. When he left thirty seconds later, the parcel was gone – even though he hadn't walked anywhere near my letterbox on entry. And there was nothing by or behind the pots to suggest the use of a safe place.

The third notable detail was what sounded like his parting words: 'Yep, got it,' spoken as he walked past my doorbell – not something one would typically say after making a delivery.

Later that day, I reviewed the footage again – slowing frames, squinting at angles, trying to read some intention into the grainy blur. But the garden gave up none of its secrets. The shadows beneath the planters stretched with measured ease, unbothered. An empty crisp packet, caught

SUCH AN ODD WORD TO USE

once more on the breeze, made its slow way across the paving stones like a stage prop that refused to exit. The sun, by then, had dipped slightly, throwing long beams through the trees as though lighting the next scene before the script had even been written.

At least two of these three new cast members seemed to follow stage directions from the wings. Yet, while their movements could be observed, their purpose remained a mystery.

Chapter 12

The Canary's Song

The events leading up to – and including – those three visits did not sit well with me. My now-discarded door-viewer camera had already malfunctioned in ways that made me question whether it had been tampered with remotely. One of those shadowy characters – whom I now thought of as 'scanners' – could have detected its presence. That might explain why it worked well for a short time, then began slipping from my control. Was I about to experience the same thing with my doorbell camera? I couldn't help but wonder if these latest visitors were acting as 'planters and retrievers' – modern-day Artful Dodgers, lifting data from cameras instead of wallets.

With evidence of something concerning taking place on private land, I felt compelled to act. I considered simply talking to Alistair. But it seemed unlikely this would lead anywhere. I suspected he might simply brush it off, using the

SUCH AN ODD WORD TO USE

opportunity to glean what I did – and, more revealingly, did not – know about his activities.

Four days later, after some research, I completed an Investigatory Powers Tribunal Complaint Form. According to Wikipedia, here's how the tribunal is described:

> *The Investigatory Powers Tribunal is a first-instance tribunal and superior court of record in the United Kingdom. It is primarily an inquisitorial court. It hears complaints about surveillance by public bodies, primarily the intelligence services. It does not hear complaints about surveillance by private bodies. It is a part of the Home Office but operates independently. It is also separate from the administration of the rest of the UK tribunals system.*

The form's 'nature of the complaint' section included a series of tick boxes. I chose the option that said that surveillance by a public authority had taken place which had resulted, or was likely to result, in private information about me being obtained.

The thought that a device was being placed and retrieved within a few feet of my home – close to my doorbell camera – was hard to dispel. The timing of these visits, six weeks after I installed the doorbell but years after I'd moved in, merely deepened my suspicion. Add to that the strange behaviour of the door viewer – the first WiFi camera I'd ever used – and it seemed plausible that someone might be trying to hack a personal device to monitor activities in that shadow-green garden.

A device I had installed for home security now felt as though it might be turned – like a double agent with a weakness waiting to be covertly exploited. If compromised, it could inform others of my comings and goings and put eyes on the visits of planning consultants, estate agents, and builders. And if it were co-opted, would I even know this time?

With a touch of whimsy, I wondered what code name my turned doorbell might be given. Perhaps Canary – perched innocently on my porch, yet singing its song to unseen ears. Somewhere, in a softly lit office cluttered with files and cold teacups, a handler might murmur under their breath, 'Canary is singing.' The day's intelligence – frames, timestamps, snippets of muffled conversations – would be neatly packaged, encrypted, and dispatched via secure channels. Somewhere along the chain, a junior operative might retrieve the file and forward it with the perfunctory note: 'Product clean. Analysis ongoing.'

And finally, Control – Alistair Greyburn in rolled-up sleeves, tobacco smoke curling above stacks of leatherbound files – would study every nuance of the postman's quite ordinary daily visit, scanning for the tell-tale signs of a builder in disguise.

Returning to less fanciful thoughts, the merits of other WiFi-enabled devices had, from time to time, crossed my

SUCH AN ODD WORD TO USE

mind. Perhaps a virtual assistant to ask if I needed an umbrella on the way out or remind me to pick up milk. But were these too potential defectors – ready to add ears to those visits, to overhear private conversations and package the product for discreet retrieval? Or, perhaps for the hell of it, send me out unprepared into a gathering storm for milk I did not need while my conspiring blinds opened and closed in Morse code. 'Dash dash dash – dot dot dash – dash,' they would signal in unison – corroborating Canary's chirping and chattering with the word 'out'. For now, smart tech was best avoided.

The odd characters I'd seen lingering around my home might not work for a public body – I was acutely aware of that. Alistair's apparent connection to at least two of those three visitors lent credence to the idea.

Some of these shadowy figures stationed themselves on the street. Others infiltrated the private front steps. At least three ventured deeper into the private communal garden. If they were deployed by a private firm, it must have been one with enviable resources – enough to keep enlisting a rotating cast of new characters.

That raised another question: funding. Even if it were a private firm, who might be paying for all this? Surely Alistair would not pay for this out of his own pocket. For those who once handled approvals no one talked about, perhaps it's not so unreasonable to wonder whether certain protections linger – quietly maintained, quietly funded. If so, how might that fit within the remit of oversight bodies such as the tribunal?

In any case, I hoped a measured complaint would, at the very least, reach him – and give him pause. I wanted an end to the steady erosion of calm. This was my only home, not a pied-à-terre to drift in and out of. I wanted to feel anchored here, not braced. And perhaps, by quietly calling out the behaviour, to leave a small marker – for myself, and for anyone else he might one day choose to unsettle.

I really liked my tucked-away house and the surrounding area. I had mixed feelings about whether or not to move. Alistair had already complicated my attempt to sell a few years earlier. Of course, as it turned out, the sale would have been derailed regardless by the issue of my home's lack of lawful residential use. I wasn't ready to try again.

At pains to stress my regard for those tasked with safeguarding national security – often behind the scenes – I completed a write-up to accompany the complaint. In another life, I could even imagine being part of that world. My concern was rooted in what I perceived to be the out-of-service behaviour of Alistair Greyburn.

The following Thursday, I returned from a coffee shop stint to find the usual vacuum lines across the upstairs carpet and the faint scent of lavender polish in the air. Marta had clearly been. The bathroom mirror, however, was slightly ajar – more than enough to notice. Nothing was out of place exactly, but something about it felt ... off. I told myself it was

SUCH AN ODD WORD TO USE

Marta's doing – a forgotten wipe-down, a cloth nudging it askew – but the thought lingered longer than it should. Perhaps I was simply attuned, by now, to the faintest shift in the pattern of things.

The complaint, signed and witnessed by a local law firm, was submitted along with the three video clips.

♪

Then I began preparing for an already-booked vacation to Turkey, now no more than a few days away. I felt sure the trip would not be as relaxing as I'd hoped. But at least I had done something.

That night, I tried to sleep, but found myself listening – to the gentle hum of the fridge, the rustle of a breeze against the eaves, the faint creak of old timber settling into silence. Everything felt veiled in stillness. As if the house itself was holding its breath.

I should have waited a few more days.

Chapter 13

The Harbingers' Echo

Five days after the third visit, and barely one day after submitting the complaint, my doorbell camera started to ignore me, then flicker obligingly back to life – barely long enough to remind me who was really in charge. My terrace-door feed followed suit.

Later that same day, I contacted the supplier. I began by explaining how reliable my little doorbell had been over the prior weeks. Then I described how it had taken to sulking like a teenager locked in their room – emerging only when it felt like it, unbothered by my authority.

The behaviour of my sulky sentry dragged on for weeks. At times it sulked in silence. At others, it tried to win back my trust with whiny excuses – blaming power cuts, accidental unplugging, or my 'temperamental' Internet connection. Like a teenager caught red-handed, it offered just enough explanation to sound plausible, but never enough to feel sincere.

And like any exasperated parent who already knows the truth but feels duty-bound to play along, I went through the motions of ruling out each excuse. I was working from home, so I knew there'd been no power cut, and I certainly hadn't unplugged the camera. The third excuse was no better. My Internet connection was solid – if it hadn't been, I'd have noticed long before the camera did.

Knowing full well it wouldn't help, I dutifully followed the supplier's all-too-familiar steps. I unplugged, rebooted, and factory reset the device with a weary inevitability.

I sent another email, this time including a screenshot showing how, after coming back online on one occasion, the recording had frozen in a zoomed-in state, oddly locked on a patch of empty brickwork – as if something had been there a moment before, or was meant to be.

I purchased a second doorbell of the same make and model to confirm what I now suspected – it was not a fault of the hardware.

I stepped back from the fresh installation and stood for a moment on the grass. It was simply a matter of ruling out more natural explanations.

From somewhere near the fig tree, a voice floated into the garden.

'It's better when you don't know who's watching.'

I turned. Lana sat cross-legged on the low stone border, sketchbook open on her lap. Her pencils were scattered beside her like fallen wands.

'That sounds ominous,' I said.

She shrugged. 'Mummy says we're all watched now. Especially the quiet ones.'

She flicked a page and began to draw again – an angular shape that looked suspiciously like my doorbell feed.

'I liked it better before it blinked all the time,' she added, almost to herself.

Then, as before, she got up and vanished behind the ivy.

So, was all this an unfortunate coincidence? And so soon after those mysterious visits? I couldn't help but feel otherwise.

Could someone have co-opted my personal device for their own purposes? Or perhaps disrupted its operation at times of their choosing? Or both? What I knew for certain was that I no longer had full control of my own doorbell camera. Nor the terrace-door camera.

I installed these devices to keep watch – yet now it felt like the stage lights had been turned back on me. I was no longer the observer but the unwitting actor, performing nightly on a set someone else had dressed.

Chapter 14

Aegean Unrest

In the few days between submitting the complaint and departing for Turkey, I sent a message to Imogen – the upstairs owner with a fascination for London's layered past. She split her time between brief visits to the flat and longer stretches elsewhere, but our trading of stories about weird incidents and the building's absurd numbering had evolved into a grounding ritual of weekly chess games – drifting at first through the airy indirection of the Réti Opening, curling inward into the watchful bristles of the Hedgehog, and now edging towards sharper, riskier lines neither of us yet named.

After the doorbell captured three unfamiliar visitors in quick succession, though, I felt this was no longer something for our usual chat window. I needed the perspective of someone who understood both the property and its history – preferably in person. We couldn't manage a catch-up before I travelled, but she promised to suggest a date and place once I was back.

With bag packed, I left my doorbell to its crotchety behaviour and headed for the sun.

♪

I stayed at a secluded resort, nestled in a lush, pine-fringed cove along the Aegean coast. I tried to relax – reading books, exercising, and enjoying the sun – but it was hard to stifle thoughts of how the complaint might play out.

While lazing deep in thought on the beach, my doorbell – when not in one of its offline stroppy moods – kept me apprised of the goings-on. 'Your front door camera's seen an unfamiliar face' it would helpfully report from time to time. Even when it was behaving, I was beginning to regret ever installing it.

Awaking from one sunbed-cradling nap, and eager to distract myself from less fruitful thoughts, I grabbed my iPad and delved back into the comings and goings of the rock bands that once graced my home. That search unearthed a surprising discovery. An old newspaper clipping reported the mysterious disappearance of a Viktor Ralston 'shortly after the recent recording sessions of Zinc Void and Desert Penguins.' It described him as the session bookings administrator for the very studio that had since become my home. Distraught colleagues were quoted recalling him as 'warm, friendly, and incredibly hard-working – often arriving long before anyone else and leaving long after'.

SUCH AN ODD WORD TO USE

Instead of providing the distraction I'd hoped for, the discovery merely deepened the mystery. An expanding cast of odd characters, and now a disappearance to boot – what exactly was going on?

Then, a day or two later, as if my doorbell sensed, and wished to compound, my unease, it delivered yet another enigmatic recording. This time, it showed Lana's mum – whom I first noticed years ago, manoeuvring a pram that gave off a faint clink with each step – stooping beside a wooden slatted garden bench of a style often found in parks. She appeared to be examining the legs and underside with a kind of uncertain diligence, one hand shading her eyes as if expecting to uncover a code or trigger. Immediately behind her stood Lana, hands on hips, her small frame pitched forward just enough to signal suspicion, her tone halfway between curiosity and accusation.

'That's where Smoky Pipe Man sits,' she declared. 'What are you *doing*?'

The woman straightened up, flustered, brushing a strand of hair from her face. 'He phoned to ask me to take a quick look at something,' she said, not quite to Lana, nor to the camera – more as if trying to convince herself.

She glanced around, half-apologetic, then led her daughter quietly back towards the flats. The whole scene was faintly theatrical, like a rehearsal for a play with no title and only the loosest direction whispered from the wings. It was almost tempting to say something, but having a doorbell address

Lana's mum from behind a tree would only have compounded the strangeness of the incident.

That evening, I stood alone on the balcony of my hotel room, drink in hand, watching the sun trail a bruised pink ribbon across the horizon. Somewhere below, a wedding band played a slow waltz to a half-listening crowd. The cicadas were winding down their daily percussion, and the breeze carried with it the scent of grilled fish and rosemary. It should have been idyllic. But my thoughts kept wandering back to Lana's mum – bent awkwardly under the wooden bench – and the unusual, reluctant shape of her explanation. I found myself wondering what, exactly, she thought she was looking for. Or if she even knew.

On the last evening of the holiday, while waiting at the airport for my flight back to London, I received another doorbell alert. Oddly, nothing seemed to be happening in the recording. However, I noticed the lights were on in the flat opposite. Perhaps the lights themselves, bursting forth at a darkened hour, had triggered the alert.

After landing early the next morning, I saw a text from Imogen suggesting we meet that day. She'd returned unexpectedly to check in on the flat, but with a new boiler being installed, she was spending a few hours at Smithfield House with her laptop and a stack of notes. Travelling back from the airport in a

SUCH AN ODD WORD TO USE

sleep-deprived state, I briefly considered suggesting another day. But I was eager to speak to someone connected to the building – someone with both context and curiosity. I replied to say I could be there by 10 a.m.

The timing of that alert, and the possibility that Alistair had resurfaced at the flat, lingered uneasily in my thoughts. Was a new scene about to unfold, requiring in-theatre stage direction?

Chapter 15

Pancakes and Paranoia

With flocks of dog-walkers routinely taking to nearby streets, one required a little extra care when heading out on foot. Most cleaned up. Some did so half-heartedly, leaving thick smudges spread wider than before. Others did not even try. I found that the quieter, more attractive tree-lined streets demanded a higher state of alert. This presented a stark choice: the noisy, fume-filled route, or the sleepier, dog-mined one. I preferred the latter, even if it required a few dodging manoeuvres along the way. Certain moist times of the year also left the pavement covered in a slippery green algae. The combined effect required restrained dodging, delicately blended with a kind of penguin-style shuffle.

Despite my travel-weakened attentiveness this particular morning, I took the more sedate route to Smithfield House. Happily, I arrived without incident.

SUCH AN ODD WORD TO USE

♪

The streets were already stirring to life – couriers with take-away coffees, a street cleaner half-listening to a tinny radio clipped to his belt, a cyclist pausing at a red light to read a message. The city, ever shifting, ever distracted. And yet I felt as though I were moving through a separate film reel, slightly out of sync with the rest of the day.

Smithfield House stood nearby – a flexible, many-faced venue on the fringe of the market. Behind its tall windows, a ground-floor brasserie eased into the day, its booths half-filled with early risers and unhurried regulars. The space struck a careful balance between business and leisure: hired rooms upstairs for meetings and celebrations – downstairs, a scattering of tables and deep-set booths, ideal for solitary work, or conversations not yet ready to be overheard.

The place was not unknown to me as I sometimes walked there for a Sunday brunch. On prior visits I had typically ordered their oatmeal porridge topped with caramelised banana, nuts, and seeds. Alongside it, I had their energy-boost smoothie, because who doesn't need more of that.

Mums and dads would enter with their child holding a balloon and gift only to be sent to an upstairs function room. If Lana had ever attended a party here, I liked to think she left behind a formal critique – perhaps taped to a helium balloon – detailing the insufficiency of glitter or the unacceptable crunch-to-fluff ratio of the cake. In the summer, all the bi-folding doors would be thrown open to the bustling street activity and noise beyond.

When I arrived that morning, Imogen was already seated in a corner booth by the window. She had one of those collapsible archive folders with her, always half-full of pamphlets and marginalia from some local collection. I hadn't seen her since her brief visit weeks earlier and was mildly relieved she'd agreed to meet. A few years younger than me, Imogen was a longtime flat owner in the building – though she mostly sublet it – and possessed a disarming curiosity for all things buried, filed, or forgotten. She had once spent three weeks reconstructing the route of a long-forgotten post-war bakery cart using only council meeting minutes and an out-of-date trade directory. I'd been, in spite of myself, captivated by the way she lit up when retelling the whole bakery-cart saga – half detective, half time traveller – and found myself picturing the kind of eccentric philanthropist who might have commissioned such a no-expense-spared sleuthing operation, perhaps with a monocle and a deep emotional investment in sourdough.

It was the kind of harmless eccentricity that briefly grounded me – until my eyes drifted to the adjacent booth. There sat a man, wearing over-ear headphones, his eyes fixed on a laptop. Given my tired state, the open question of what the complaint might trigger, and what I regarded as the likely presence of Alistair Greyburn back in his flat that very morning, I felt as though I were teetering on DEFCON 2. In such a state of mind, suspicion came easily – every glance a redacted report, every silence a veiled signal.

♪

Having not eaten anything in a while, I ordered pancakes and a latte from a young Colombian waitress whom I had come to know quite well over previous visits. After a little small talk, and fuelled by the pancakes with maple syrup, I set to my purpose. As I began recounting the story to Imogen, I noticed subtle shifts in laptop-guy's facial expressions. It almost seemed as though he were responding to what I was saying. Was this a figment of my imagination – fed by exhaustion and heightened vigilance? Quite possibly.

I described what I had seen in the clips of the three visits, explaining too what was happening off-camera during the second. She agreed the behaviour appeared suspicious and said it wouldn't be out of the question for it to be private-sector work, possibly ex-military. She also asked if I thought Alistair's actions were 'deliberately destabilising'. I said I found them 'controlling'. She nodded, thoughtful. When she asked if he might be aware of the complaint, I was momentarily drawn back to those recent alerts – the light, the bench, the timing. 'It wouldn't surprise me,' I said, the words quieter than I meant them to be.

By the end of our conversation, I felt a little more at ease, having shared my concerns and actions with someone I trusted – someone accustomed to the oddities that live uneasily in the margins. Now I just had to await the outcome of the complaint.

Chapter 16

A Shot Across the Bow

Amid the uncertainty at home, work remained its own small realm of structure. The project had entered a new phase: short-listing titles for final line-ups, adapting editorial notes across languages, and liaising with legal teams over last-minute rights clarifications. Most days, I began with a spreadsheet and ended with a call – Tokyo before breakfast, Toronto after lunch. Each conversation required a subtle recalibration of tone. One country might favour politically edged literary fiction – another preferred intimate memoirs. My role was to harmonise without erasing, to nudge and shape. It kept my hours full – and my mind, if not entirely at ease, at least usefully occupied.

Almost four weeks after meeting up with Imogen, I received the tribunal's response via my solicitor.

In short, they said its members had carefully reviewed my application and found it to be clearly unsustainable – that is to say that it had no chance of success. They dismissed the complaint. They further advised that no appeal was allowed under UK law. And with regret, they informed me they would not enter into any further correspondence on the matter.

Oddly, I felt something closer to relief than dissatisfaction. My intent had simply been to fire a warning shot across the prow of Alistair Greyburn's creeping surveillance craft. I wanted it out of my waters. No more than that.

Maybe the three visitors were sent by a private firm. Or perhaps the tribunal thought my complaint lacked sufficient weight. After all, it didn't directly link these visits to the securing of private information. The loss of control over my cameras happened *after* I'd made the complaint. And I had not made any mention of the out-of-control door-viewer device. Either, or both, might explain why my complaint had been dismissed.

I now suspected, more firmly than before, that Alistair was aware of the complaint. Nothing was said, but his body language over the days that followed seemed to radiate barely contained satisfaction. There would be a small burst of activity in front of my doorbell: pots brought into the garden for a jolly good noisy scraping, and rear windows polished with the precision of soldiers preparing for Trooping the Colour.

On one occasion, as a bemused tenant swept out from the hallway behind the racing green door, I recall Alistair – chest

SUCH AN ODD WORD TO USE

faintly puffed, steps measured – appearing a little beyond his own threshold and asking, 'Everything under control?' It struck me as oddly pointed, so different from the usual 'How are you?' There was something in his phrasing – *control* – so soon after I'd used the same word at Smithfield House. Perhaps it was nothing. A small coincidence. But it lingered all the same.

The doorbell continued its sulky, erratic behaviour. So, around this time, I decided to delete my account and abandoned what had once been a diligent and reliable little device – one that so faithfully serves millions of doors around the world.

The protective line had dissolved. The king was alone now, his court dispersed – the quiet order of the opening gone.

Much later, I would replace the doorbell – with a new one that looked like a tiny round flying saucer crash-landed into the wet paint of my porch wall, unable to free itself, glowing eerily through the night as if vainly signalling its home planet, broadcasting distress over a botched invasion attempt on a civilisation of the wrong scale, and wearily resigned to its new duties as a doorbell.

I allowed myself a flicker of cautious hope that a line had, at last, been drawn in the sand.

Chapter 17

Predictable Prey

Since moving to the area, I had asked but a few women out on dates. Among them were a French restaurant manager, a Spanish dentist who once repaired a troublesome tooth, and a Czech woman I met during a popular fitness class run by former military personnel in Clissold Park.

I rarely brought anyone home and put little effort into dating. I felt quite content with the solitary life I had grown accustomed to over the years. Hidden away as I was in an otherwise bustling metropolis, I think I liked the dichotomy of it. Time seemed to fly by as I absorbed myself deeply in various projects.

One of my quieter obsessions was chess – not the playing of it so much as the study, though I'd now settled into a weekly game with Imogen. I became fascinated by positions in which attack masked defence, and defence concealed a latent counter-strike. My miniature boards at home played host to these static dramas, each one arrested mid-manoeuvre, as though time itself had paused to consider the next move. The house

SUCH AN ODD WORD TO USE

became a theatre of suspended tension, each board a different act. In retrospect, I think I took comfort in these locked positions – scenarios where all the pieces were visible, the rules known, the motives legible. Real life, as I was discovering, offered no such clarity.

There's a particular reason I mention all this. Before describing what follows, I should say – I am straight. I mention it only because, from the outside, it might not have been obvious, given my contentment with solitude and lack of visible romantic entanglements. I've always found it easy to lose myself in self-contained pursuits and rarely feel the need for social or intimate connection.

On weekdays, tethered by work, I rarely ventured far from the house. But on weekends, I had regular – and occasionally farther-flung – haunts for a relaxed breakfast with the papers. One particular Sunday favourite, now sadly closed, sat along a beautiful street lined with floral façades, colourful cafés, and elegant shops. I frequented it for several years.

During earlier visits, I'd connect to their WiFi to read the digital Sunday papers. After some months, I noticed multiple networks bearing the café's name – each with a unique suffix. The staff told me only one was legitimate. Had someone set up another network nearby with the same name and password? From then on, I resolved to download the papers before setting out and began to avoid public WiFi altogether.

On one visit, I sat on a stool at the short bar facing the window – my usual spot. The staff knew my order without asking, and I could occasionally distract myself by watching people stroll past the shops, unbothered by weekday stress.

A young woman sat next to me and struck up a conversation. Her demeanour felt overly earnest, as though trying too hard to keep the interaction alive. Her body language too betrayed a flicker of unease – an occasional glance away, an overly deliberate smile. Maybe she was simply nervous. Maybe I was over-interpreting. But after thousands of coffee shop visits, you develop a certain instinct for what feels natural and what doesn't.

I kept my responses polite but measured. When she left, her expression carried the faintest shadow of disappointment – perhaps the scent of mission failure.

Months later, something similar happened – this time with a man, in the same café. I'd chosen a communal table in an adjoining room, flanked by benches.

First, a couple entered and perched on stools across the room, facing the wall. Something about them felt off. The man studied the menu with his back to me – the woman angled herself at forty-five degrees, seemingly keeping me in her peripheral vision while briefly tapping her phone. They completely ignored each other.

A moment later, another man walked in and seated himself directly opposite me at the narrow communal table. He placed his gloves conspicuously within my line of sight. Dressed in a style similar to my own – winter clothes anchored by a black

SUCH AN ODD WORD TO USE

roll neck jumper – he told the waitress he wasn't ready to order because he was waiting for someone.

Something about this did not feel right. I finished my coffee earlier than I'd intended and got up to put on my coat. Then roll-neck blurted out a question about my iPad – a question chosen with the urgency of someone fumbling for the nearest object in a dark room. It seemed like a desperate attempt to engage in conversation over something so commonplace. And it was so abrupt that I recall others at the communal table and on neighbouring tables suddenly looking around as if plates of food had smashed on the floor.

I muttered something about it being great for reading the Sunday papers and made a beeline for the cash desk, settled up and left.

At the time, it struck me as feeling possibly arranged and coordinated. If someone wanted to place a friend – an asset – in someone else's life with whom they might confide, or coax them into joining a network you controlled, then finding a relatively remote café that one could be sure would be reliably frequented on a given day and at a given time, would be an effective way to do it. And if they didn't know how best to play it, then trying both a female and a male approach would increase their odds.

Someone might even be sent in first to scout the space, or discreetly signal where the second person should sit – ensuring the approach seemed as organic as possible.

87

Could I have misread all this? Perhaps. But given the preceding chain of events, it felt real enough to unsettle me. And it didn't stop. What lingered later was how concentrated it had all been – two strange, overly deliberate encounters, and a baffling proliferation of suspect networks – all centred on that one café, in that one tucked-away corner of the city, at exactly the time I was known to appear. Nowhere else during that period. Just there.

Months later, walking down that same street, I noticed the café had closed for good. The windows were papered over. No sign. No explanation. Simply gone – as if the final act had played out and the set quietly dismantled.

On one of my daily walks to the canal, I noticed someone standing on the corner across the road, holding a phone to their ear. The moment I noticed them, they turned their back to me.

When I reached the end of the street and turned the corner, they turned as well, appearing to follow me from the opposite side of the road, still talking on the phone. Out of caution, I walked past the canal entrance instead of entering. Glancing back, I saw the person had stopped near the entrance, still talking.

Assuming it was nothing, I crossed the road, doubled back, and took the steps down to the canal. As I walked along the canal path, I saw the same person on the phone walking along the path on the other side, only steps behind.

When I quickened my pace, so did they.

I couldn't shake the feeling of being followed. I couldn't help but wonder if they were noting my absence from home. Was something happening back there? Or was it yet another coincidence? It wasn't entirely wild imagination – after all, there had been clear prior incidents caught on camera. Whatever the case, I cut my usual route short and headed back.

Unusual incidents like these often appeared in small clusters, followed by months of relative calm before anything unusual, at least anything I observed, happened again. This pattern gave me greater confidence that I was witnessing something real. Had these events been a figment of my imagination, surely they would not have been so tightly clustered. Would paranoia be so discerning?

For quite some time, one coffee shop in Exmouth Market was my regular lunchtime destination. I'd stay for about twenty minutes or so on weekdays, maybe a bit longer on weekends.

I recall one day sitting in one of two armchairs near the front. Behind the adjacent sofa, there was space for patrons to pass through. Two men entered and stood there, hunched over a single phone facing me. One gestured towards me, as though seeking the other's approval. Moments later, a third man entered, bypassed the counter entirely, and politely asked if he could sit beside me.

The déjà vu was unmistakable. I finished my coffee and left.

After this series of occurrences – whether real or imagined – I began varying my routine. I later stopped taking daily walks along the canal and altered my routes to be a little less predictable.

I sometimes imagined the odd characters fading back into the crowd – masks peeled, wires tucked away – returning to flats or vans or job titles that never quite matched their actions. The café stayed open, the canal lapped softly at its edges, and no one seemed to notice the subtle pulse beneath the surface.

Chapter 18

The Wet Room

The city held its secrets – but so, it turned out, did my bathroom.

It was early in the year of Covid when I contacted a design company about converting it into a wet room. That same day, the Foreign and Commonwealth Office issued its advisory against all travel to China's Hubei Province. It all felt so far away.

With just one bathroom in my small house, I booked two weeks' holiday for early March to ensure the work could be done in my absence. My plan was to stay at one of London's Soho Houses, a favourite of mine for their blend of homeliness and indulgence. The setting offered the perfect balance: a space conducive to relaxation and, with my laptop in tow, the pursuit of a personal project. Their distinctive décor often inspired the vision for my own spaces – my wet room, in fact, was to be modelled on one I'd used during a previous stay, complete with a shelfie of colourful Cowshed shower gels.

By 5th March, everything was in place. The designer confirmed the work would begin early the following week, and I was set to decamp to Soho House. That same day, the BBC announced the UK's first Covid death, with cases surpassing 100. The national focus began to shift – 'delay' was replacing 'containment'.

I asked the company to complete the work by the 20th, ensuring my return to a functional bathroom. Yet, as the days passed, the bathroom itself began to feel like a secondary concern. By 9th March, the FTSE 100 suffered its sharpest plunge since 2008, and Italy entered lockdown.

By 16th March, one week into my stay, the UK death toll reached 55, with cases surpassing 1,500. The Prime Minister urged people to work from home and avoid social venues wherever possible. I called the installers to ask whether the toilet was operational so I could return home. Meanwhile, the Soho House venue, though growing emptier by the day, remained open. The workmen informed me they were still chasing out the floor to fit a recessed shower tray.

Two days later, the urgency to return home became undeniable. The pound had plunged to its lowest level against the dollar since 1985. Deaths had surpassed 100, and the government announced that all schools would close by the end of the week. A UK lockdown now felt inevitable, following in Italy's footsteps.

Arriving home, I found my bathroom reduced to an empty shell. The materials were on site, the flooring prepared, and,

SUCH AN ODD WORD TO USE

mercifully, the toilet functional. Now, the race was on to complete the shower while work remained permissible.

It was then that events took a mysterious turn. As the final tiles were being stripped from the walls, one was found to conceal a hidden compartment. The craftsmanship was extraordinary – held in place by a magnetic seal and grouted so seamlessly it was visually indistinguishable from its neighbours. Even when reattached and tapped, the tile gave nothing away. It was a marvel of concealment. To access the compartment, one would first need to know exactly which of the hundreds of tiles to target and then painstakingly remove the surrounding grout to enable the breaking of the seal.

The compartment itself was mystery enough. But what lay within proved even more beguiling: a small Filofax, a quintessential relic of the 1980s. Its sleek, slightly weathered black leather cover bore the marks of hurried handling. The softened corners seemed to trace a cryptic map of its well-thumbed history. The tarnished nickel clasp, faintly scratched, hinted at moments of inspiration – or urgency. Inside, the crisp ivory pages were lined not with mundane appointments, but with musical staves. Each sheet overflowed with intricate notations, fragments of melodies, and what appeared to be carefully composed riffs – all tantalisingly incomplete.

The A–Z tabs, glossy yet slightly dog-eared, hinted at a meticulous mind at work amid the bursts of creativity. Yet the arrangement of the notes felt eerily intentional – an uncanny precision in the patterns that suggested a rhythm beyond mere music. The Filofax exuded a faint, evocative aroma of ink and aged leather, mingled with the lingering trace of tobacco. Even the tabs seemed carefully considered: only B, H, J, K, L, M, N, P, T, and W were present.

At first glance, it seemed to be the private chronicle of a musician – a diary of experimentation and inspiration. As a teenager, I played piano and guitar to a respectable grade, and though my musical knowledge had long since faded, I couldn't help but notice something unusual in the arrangement of these notes. For a fleeting moment, I wondered if I was holding a fragment of music history – perhaps the early sketches of a great band testing the waters of their craft. Yet there was an unease in the precision of those staves, a subtle suggestion that their purpose stretched well past melody.

For now, though, more immediate concerns demanded attention. With the spectre of lockdown looming, securing a functioning shower had become paramount. The alternative – weeks, perhaps even months, washing at the kitchen sink – was far from appealing.

By 23rd March, the bathroom was operational. There were minor snags, but nothing urgent. I could shower. I could use the loo. That evening, Boris Johnson announced a nationwide lockdown.

SUCH AN ODD WORD TO USE

And so, as the country retreated into isolation, I found myself alone with my newly transformed wet room – and the enigma of the Filofax.

After settling into a new routine to fill the cloistered hours and distract myself from the world outside, my thoughts drifted back to that little black notebook. I opened it at the well-filled M section. The first three staves of the opening sheet caught my attention – there was something strangely disjointed about them. I tried humming the notes, but they sounded dreadful. I couldn't decide whether my long-dormant musical skills were to blame or if the composition itself was genuinely awful. Perhaps both. Why would someone go to such meticulous lengths to commit something so discordant to paper? And more puzzling still, why go to such effort to conceal it?

Each time I opened that notebook in the weeks that followed, it put my head in a chokehold. Every attempt to make sense of its contents felt like my mind wrestling itself into submission. The one concrete detail I managed to glean – thanks to the conveniently annotated dates – was that the sheets had been composed over several years, amid an era of faxed contracts, dial-up tones, and badly dubbed demo tapes. Though, given the quality of the music, 'decomposed' felt like the better term.

There were no more than five distinct dates, mostly grouped by section. For instance, all the sheets for one particular year were filed under M or B, and nowhere else.

Yet M also contained a few stray sheets from later years, as if deliberately misplaced – or perhaps previously overlooked.

There's a kind of magic in how the mind embraces a thorny challenge, working away in the background without your slightest awareness, only to surprise you one morning with the fruits of its labour. Perhaps it had been nudged into action by a passage in a novel or a scene in a film. Whatever the spark, I found myself reaching for that notebook with a renewed sense of vigour.

It took several more weeks of toil, but I felt as giddy as a child with a new toy. It reminded me of those childhood days spent assembling and painting a model aircraft carrier – moments when any interruption was unthinkable, even if it meant pushing my bladder well past the red zone on the need-to-pee dial. Those weeks flew by in a blur of fascination and determination.

It revealed itself as a book of secrets hidden in plain sight. Each stave was a self-contained cypher. Every letter of the alphabet was mapped to a note on the chromatic scale, extended over three octaves to encompass all twenty-six letters. To lend those notes an appearance of realism and melody, their lengths nudged certain notes up or down by one or two half-steps. The rests held no significance – merely a device to standardise bar lengths and give the score a natural appearance. The result? A seemingly innocent snippet of music concealing a coded message.

SUCH AN ODD WORD TO USE

To a trained ear, these snippets would be dismissed as inconsequential fragments. To an untrained ear, they would mean nothing at all – leaving merely the beauty of the notebook itself to be admired.

But when I applied the method in full, the first names began to emerge – *Lucas Tremblay, Nathan Reid, Alina Singh* – each line of music yielding a life once hidden.

I could find no historical or literary precedent for a specific cypher system quite like this one. Musical cyphers as a broader category were not unheard of. I recalled reading that Johann Sebastian Bach famously embedded the musical cryptogram B-A-C-H (the German notation for B flat, A, C, B natural) into his compositions as a kind of signature. Yet this particular system seemed wholly unique – a carefully crafted enigma, standing apart from known examples.

When an answer breeds questions like rabbits, you know the real story is just beginning. Who crafted these cyphers, and why? What did that reduced set of lettered sections signify? If every stave concealed a name, then there must have been close to two hundred – who were they?

Though this episode seemed curiously disconnected from all prior incidents, surveillance and cyphers were not the most improbable of bedfellows. And my house, in ways yet to be explained, appeared to be the common thread that bound them.

Chapter 19

Lana's Interlude

In the wake of that peculiar discovery, I found myself drawn back to smaller, steadier things. The days that followed were among the most gently restorative I'd spent at the house. Not because anything momentous happened – far from it. But something had shifted. I'd arranged the table and chairs, settled the pots into place, added a few familiar plants. The rooftop terrace, once the focus of contention and endless admin, now felt settled, dignified. It became what I'd always hoped: a modest private perch with a good view and a little space to think.

I took to reading there in the late afternoon, sunlight warming the deck boards and a gentle breeze stirring the potted herbs. I even treated myself to a beanbag, at the suggestion of Lana, who had quite suddenly become the neighbourhood's self-appointed authority on rooftop comfort.

I happened to glance up from my deck chair and spotted Lana observing from an upstairs window. Her small figure was framed by the tall sash with its slender glazing bars, elbows

SUCH AN ODD WORD TO USE

resting on the sill, chin lifted in a posture of quiet appraisal. The next time I passed her in the garden, she leaned in conspiratorially and whispered, 'I saw the beanbag. Good choice.' I thanked her with mock solemnity, and she gave an approving nod, as if conferring some official neighbourhood seal.

It was around that time that I began to notice her spending more time outside, often crouched on the garden path with a pad of paper and an overflowing pencil tin. Sometimes she used a clipboard – at other times, a patch of cardboard as a makeshift desk. At first, I assumed it was some school assignment – mapping plant life or designing an ideal tree house. I'd offer a passing wave, and she'd give a distracted thumbs-up or squint at me as if I were interrupting a code-breaking session.

Then one Saturday, I saw her out early. The garden was still wet with dew, and she was marking something on a large folded sheet with small, deliberate crosses. As I approached with a watering can, she hastily turned the paper over and sat on it.

'Top secret?' I asked.

'Almost,' she said without looking up.

I smiled and left her to it.

A few days later, I returned from the shops and found her in the same spot, this time adjusting a compass tool as she peered at the reclaimed paving stones. She muttered something about 'alignment' and 'angles of approach', and again turned the paper over when she caught me watching.

I said nothing, but my curiosity was piqued.

CARL GOODWIN

♪

The next interruption came not from above, like her watchful glance from the window, but at ground level. Late one morning, I heard a sharp rapping at the door – three quick knocks, as if from someone who'd thought better of it but knocked anyway. I opened it to find Lana, slightly flushed, clutching a half-eaten apple in one hand and a pink stick of chalk in the other.

'You need to come out. Right now,' she said.

'Is something wrong?'

'No. But it's ready.'

She took off down the path before I could ask what *it* was. Intrigued, I followed, stepping into the brightness of the leafy garden.

Ahead of the bench, across one of the smoother stretches of paving, she had drawn a hopscotch grid. But instead of numbers, each square bore a phrase in uneven block letters: *safe step*, *not yet*, *spy leaf*, *don't wave here*, *check again*, *quick feet only*. The final square – larger than the others – was simply marked with a spiral.

'Hopscotch?' I ventured.

'Sort of,' she said, balancing on one foot at the start. 'But the garden decides the rules.'

She launched into the sequence – deliberate, silent, placing her feet with exaggerated care. At *spy leaf* she paused, adjusted her stance, then skipped forward two squares. At

SUCH AN ODD WORD TO USE

don't wave here, she crouched low and covered her face with her arms.

'What happens if you step wrong?'

'Depends,' she said, brushing her hands on her shorts. 'Mostly you have to go back and try again. But sometimes something sees you.'

I smiled, though her tone gave me pause. 'And the names?'

She looked up. 'Just what the garden says. I listen.'

A breeze stirred through the branches. One of the chalk letters smudged slightly. Lana didn't seem to mind.

'You can try if you want,' she offered, stepping aside.

I hesitated, then gave a theatrical sigh. 'I should warn you, I once failed a hopscotch test in Year 3. I might set off all the wrong leaves.'

She grinned. 'You just have to listen.'

I nodded. 'All right. But only if I'm allowed a practice round – with a spotter.'

'Deal.'

After a flailing attempt that left me wobbling through *spy leaf* and completely botching *don't wave here*, I stepped back, faintly embarrassed. But the feeling dissolved the moment I looked up and saw her face – lit with the kind of joy that made even my gracelessness feel like part of the magic. It was as if the garden had approved, and she was its delighted envoy.

Later that day, passing along the side path, I caught a glimpse of her at the garden table, her pencil tin open and scraps of paper weighed down with stones. She was adding something to a larger sheet, using a stubby brown pencil to shade around the outline of a tree. Her head tilted slightly, as if the light had to hit the paper just right for her to see the lines. From time to time, she glanced towards my porch, then back at the paper.

It looked like a game. But there was something in her focus – careful, intent, unshowy – that stayed with me long after she disappeared indoors.

♪

That evening, I sat on the roof, the fading light slipping through the narrow uprights of the black wrought iron railing. Below, the garden settled into its twilight hush, branches swaying gently above the mulch and moss. The last remnants of chalk lingered on a patch of compacted earth near the clearing – a faint hopscotch grid, its enigmatic labels half-faded but still legible in the low light.

Lana's game stayed with me – the chalked instructions, the careful steps, the small coded gestures. And now, that earlier glimpse of her at the garden table, lost in concentration over a patchwork of papers. It no longer felt like a school project. There was something else in the way she worked – precise and unhurried, as if tracing connections only she could see.

Of all the things one might draw in a garden – flowers, trees, squirrels – it was the less innocent presences, the small

SUCH AN ODD WORD TO USE

behaviours, the ones that whispered rather than announced, that seemed to have caught her attention most.

Her mother appeared at the kitchen window with a tray of washing-up. Lana dashed inside. A minute later, the hush returned to the rooms above.

I thought of asking her what she was working on. Maybe even seeing if she needed more paper. But somehow, I knew better. Whatever it was, it was still in progress. A living document of sorts – half-game, half-watching brief – and besides, I suspected she hadn't shown me everything.

I leaned back in the beanbag – her approved beanbag – and let the last of the sun warm my face.

There had been so many characters, real and ambiguous, these past few years. I had notebooks of my own. But somehow, whatever Lana was making – dense with whimsy and sharp observation – felt closer to the truth than anything I could manage in ten thousand words.

And now I found myself wondering what she might draw next. What I'd taken for a school task turned out to be something far more ambitious – a whimsical prelude to a deeper kind of noticing.

Chapter 20

An Unwitting Pawn

Marta continued her Thursday afternoon visits, usually while I slipped off to a coffee shop to avoid getting underfoot. She cleaned with meticulous care and, on her way out, carried the bin bags to the store by the side gate – one for general waste, one for recycling. I'd come back to the faint scent of lavender polish and the gentle sheen of a freshly mopped concrete floor, only occasionally returning without having seen her at all.

Bins were collected early on Mondays and Thursdays. So, the bin store rarely had anything other than my rubbish in it prior to Sunday night.

I recall one Thursday evening when Alistair was in residence. I was pottering about in the garden tidying the area around my porch. It was already dusk. I noticed Alistair near the side path, wearing yellow household gloves and crouched next to the open

SUCH AN ODD WORD TO USE

bin store, seemingly rummaging inside a bin bag. It caught my attention but could have been entirely innocent.

It struck me then that my bin bags – left unattended for four nights a week – might contain all sorts of private information: perhaps details of a holiday booking, scribbled notes about a potential planning application, or even a carelessly discarded window remote. From that moment, I resolved never to leave anything of significance in either bag.

Marta liked to listen to music through a pair of lightweight, rose-gold Beats headphones while she worked. It was only after several years that she asked – very politely – if she could use my WiFi. I wasn't sure why she hadn't mentioned it before, nor, come to think of it, why I'd never offered. My router supported a guest network for exactly that purpose, and I had only recently enabled it, so no one else had access. I set up her phone to connect.

A couple of weeks later, while working on my laptop at a nearby coffee shop, I received an alert from my router: someone was attempting to use a Virtual Private Network on the guest WiFi. A VPN is perfectly sensible on public networks – it masks your device's IP address and encrypts your traffic. But having initially used the guest network without one, it wasn't clear why there was now a need for one on a trusted private connection, simply to stream music.

By this point, my imagination had begun drifting into more unsettling territory. Marta had told me she'd recently taken on a new client. Was it possible she had been, entirely innocently, nudged into using VPNs across her cleaning jobs? An insignificant habit, softly introduced, under the guise of online safety?

I wasn't suggesting anything deliberate on her part – far from it. If anything, I worried for her – how easily small, kind acts could be secretly appropriated. But my mind, shaped by months of disquieting encounters, had started constructing cautious scenarios – even ones I didn't fully believe.

I could almost hear the exchange now – friendly, practical, disarming:

'Would you like to use our WiFi while you're here? You must be using a lot of data to download music.'

'Oh – yes, that would be great.'

'Have you asked your other clients? Might be useful for streaming or calling your daughter on a break.'

'That's a lovely idea. Thank you.'

And perhaps, on a later visit:

'You should be careful though – public networks aren't always safe. You should install a VPN. I'll send you a link.'

A small kindness, offered with just enough concern to mask a deeper intent. One tap on a link. One simple habit reshaped.

Could that new client have been someone working for a private security firm – someone in need of a reliable cleaner?

SUCH AN ODD WORD TO USE

One of the exhibits in my statutory declaration, which had been publicly available for quite some time, was a headed letter from Marta. Might her phone have been unknowingly leveraged as a cutout to access my network? The idea seemed far-fetched and likely improbable. Yet, given the strange events I'd experienced, it was difficult to dismiss entirely.

I declined the VPN request. The router had flagged it early, and I'd shut it down immediately. That should have ended it – at least, I hoped so. I updated the firmware soon after, more as a precaution than a cure. But some nagging instinct lingered: if something had already slipped through the door, would I even know? I told myself I was being cautious, not paranoid. But sometimes the distinction felt as thin as the guest password itself.

Marta, for her part, seemed blissfully unaware of any issue. She continued working to her usual rhythm, headphones on, occasionally humming along to a familiar tune. Watching her that day, I felt a gentle wave of protectiveness – an urge to shield her from the kind of subtle intrusion that might co-opt an everyday kindness without her ever knowing.

Perhaps because of that very feeling, it didn't seem worth risking that she might be exploited in some way. I'd been sensing, for some time, a subtle shift in both our routines – as if life was nudging us towards a change neither of us quite wanted to voice. So when I finally brought it up, I did so gently, more by feeling than design. Marta took it well, her response measured and kind. She said she'd been wondering whether the journey was still worthwhile – me being by far the client she had to travel farthest to reach – and agreed it might be time.

We parted with warmth and kept in touch.

There had been something quietly human about our long arrangement – its rhythm, its ordinariness, the way it anchored the weeks. After Marta stopped coming, Thursdays felt different somehow. Lighter, yes, but also a touch more solitary.

Still, perhaps solitude was the point. More than ever, I was learning to rely on myself – not merely for cleaning, but for protection, perspective, and peace of mind.

I now have an even greater appreciation for all the work she did, having taken on the task myself. I recall the words Marta used after I reconfigured my small bathroom into a fully tiled wet room, mostly white, in a clean-lined pattern that seemed modern at the time – and hopelessly impractical ever since. Something about style over practicality. She was right. As I regularly scrub the seemingly endless lines of grout to remove a persistent orange residue, I've come to understand exactly what she meant.

I now treat cleaning as a mini workout – a particularly helpful mindset, given that another element of my life, weekly gym visits, had also fallen by the wayside.

Shortly after I parted ways with Marta, I noticed an uptick in leaflets offering a reliable local service left in my postbox. It was most likely one of those unrelated quirks of timing. I was

SUCH AN ODD WORD TO USE

quite happy with my new regime. And if I ever did need assistance, perhaps for a one-off deep clean, it would not now be in response to unsolicited flyers. Like emails promising a miraculous inheritance, they were not to be trusted.

Chapter 21

Pull-Ups and Eaves Drops

I moved through the years the way I moved through gyms – in phases, always looking for a better fit. Initially, I trained at the local branch of an established chain close by. Later, I moved to a gym near the tube station. A more upmarket health club, requiring a more determined walk, followed that. With each change came a renewed motivation. I think I liked escaping routines and habits almost as comfortably as I fell into them.

At the first, I trained with Amelia, who later introduced me to a running club organised by a neighbouring sports outfitter. I changed at the gym, then waited in the shop for a small group to gather. There were a few regulars augmented by one or two occasional participants. Once the last customer had left, the owner locked up, and we all headed out for a brisk run along the canal lasting a little less than an hour.

SUCH AN ODD WORD TO USE

In winter, those first few moments were always the hardest – the sharp bite of cold air, shivering outside the shop, waiting for a pause in the early evening traffic. But once we set off, chattering thawed into easy chatting, and then we gradually strung ourselves out naturally according to ability, each settling into our own rhythm for the main stretch. Amelia often joined those runs. Over time, we became friends and, as is common with trainer–client relationships, we shared the day-to-day goings-on in our respective lives.

Years later, after that gym closed, I occasionally bumped into Amelia. At first, she trained clients privately. Later, she swapped kettlebells for cuffs and joined what she fondly called the bizzies. During those brief chance encounters, she sometimes reminded me of the legged-it light bulb that had so mystified me – and so thoroughly amused her.

'Still dodging trouble?' she once asked, with a wink. 'Or your electrics still got a cob on?'

I hadn't realised how much I'd missed that irreverent charm.

In more recent years, I trained at a smaller basement studio dedicated to personal training. Just off Great Sutton Street, it was hidden away without fanfare, down some steps. I knew the trainer from a previous gym membership. Along with a couple of mates, she had established a thriving business which operated solely by word of mouth.

During Covid I exercised at home. My house was perfect for this purpose. I had space to swing a kettlebell, and as a detached house rather than a flat, the unshared walls and solid concrete floor ensured I disturbed no one. The central column of my spiral staircase was ideal for attaching a suspension trainer. The double-height ceiling provided enough room to use a skipping rope. With resistance bands and similar equipment, I had a perfectly serviceable little gym.

Outside of lockdowns, there would typically be only two or three trainer–client pairs in the gym at any given time. Between the *three-sets-of-ten-of-this* and the *three-sets-of-ten-of-that*, my trainer would fill the pauses with anecdotes about her family life or the latest incident with her partner. Everyone has their trials and tribulations. It's sometimes easy to forget that when you're caught up in your own.

Like the workouts themselves, our chats followed a quiet, predictable rhythm – the small beats of ordinary life: a show she'd started, a holiday loosely pencilled in, the latest quirk from home that defied explanation but asked to be told.

Occasionally, earlier clients were mentioned in passing. For instance, there might be a brief comment about the Italian businessman she'd trained before me. Or the American lawyer who cancelled again at the last minute and would be out of the country the following week.

More recently, part way through a workout, I was talking about something or other when I noticed a client hanging

SUCH AN ODD WORD TO USE

around. They were sitting on a bench nearby, clearly listening to the conversation.

My weekly Sunday session was usually around 3 p.m., though it sometimes shifted slightly. Over time, I became increasingly aware that this same client would always have the session either immediately before or after mine.

At the end of the hour, most clients were only too eager to escape to less strenuous pursuits such as eating or socialising. But this particular client, if they trained before me, would stick around. They seemed to be using, but not really using, a nearby piece of equipment. The equipment wasn't intended for unsupervised use. Space was limited, and the entire model rested on one-to-one training.

If they had the slot after me, my trainer might, I suspected, sometimes make innocent remarks, such as, 'Mark's away on vacation for the next two weeks, so we could do an hour earlier if you want.' These were the kind of casual, innocent remarks – entirely unrelated to anything else – that I would hear myself about the person who trained before me.

I couldn't shake the unease that this client was less a fellow gym-goer and more a mobile listening device, positioned at a place where I could be reliably found at a specific time. Even if there was only a small chance this was true, the niggling discomfort was becoming a constant presence.

Had I been more adept at deception, I might have laid a subtle trail of disinformation – small, intentional inaccuracies to test my suspicions. The idea brought to mind George

Smiley's patient unravelling of the Circus mole in *Tinker Tailor Soldier Spy*. In the end, I simply changed my workout day. Looking back, I wonder why I hadn't done so sooner – it meant I could finally catch the live Sunday afternoon football.

After I switched days, I half-expected to see the same client appear at my new time slot – an echo following me across the calendar. But they didn't. It was a strangely anticlimactic relief, like finding no message in a bottle after weeks of watching the tide.

Later, seeking to save a few pennies, I decided to stop personal training sessions altogether and revert to my battle-tested routines of exercising at home.

Instead of the one-hour weekly sessions I had reduced myself to in recent years, I began doing fifteen to twenty minutes of exercise each day. To me, those one-hour sessions had always seemed more about convenience and revenue than truly responding to the body's needs. I enjoyed the idea of these shorter, sharper sessions at the end of the day, followed by an earned shower.

I recall seeing this episode as a wholly positive turn of events at the time. Yet, in further distancing myself from interactions, I sense now the creeping quietness of withdrawal from life.

Chapter 22

A Façade Restored

During an autumn that lingered like late summer, badly needed work began on renovating the main Georgian building. It had long worn the weathered look of a place trying to outlast its own reputation – its fluted pilasters chipped and crumbling at the corners, like icing giving way on an over-warmed cake. The fanlight above the entrance door bore a hairline crack through its etched sunburst, and one loose pane in the transom occasionally clicked when the wind changed. Paint flaked from the once-grand racing green door, revealing the bare wood beneath in veined streaks, as if time itself had begun to peel back the building's skin.

Round the back, through the narrow hallway, the rear of the building fared little better. Here, the original back door – solid, panelled, and handsomely proportioned – had sagged slightly on its hinges, resisting each push with the weary groan of a reluctant confidant. A rusting bell-pull hung to one side, disconnected from anything at all, though it still moved faintly in strong wind. Ivy crept from the garden wall towards the upper windows like a cautious intruder, emboldened by the years of inattention.

The scaffolding, when it arrived, was almost elegant in comparison – neat towers front and back, joined by planks and netting that fluttered like theatre curtains on dress rehearsal day. Even the skips, when delivered, were neatly aligned. Something orderly had begun to form, though it came with the faint impression that the building itself, having been left to decline for so long, was now slightly wary of the sudden affection. Or perhaps it was simply unused to such attention.

As work got underway, it soon became clear that Alistair had assumed the role of informal foreman, orchestrating progress with measured authority. At regular intervals, he appeared to consult with the lead contractor – gesturing here, pointing there, gently steering attention towards this snag or that imperfection. His presence, though not official, was undeniably influential.

I recall one instance in the moss-softened garden: Alistair and the contractor deep in conversation, their gazes eventually rising to study the upper floors. Alistair then subtly

SUCH AN ODD WORD TO USE

retreated, aligning his back with the wall of my home – right beside my softly glowing, flying-saucer-like doorbell. A few days later, the scene repeated almost exactly, though this time he took up position on the other side of the doorbell. The symmetry was near-perfect, like blocking cues in a muted drama known only to its cast.

On rare occasions, there might be a direct encounter with Alistair.

'Any plans to go away?' he'd casually ask.

What would happen while I was away? I wondered.

'Nothing planned,' I would reply.

Weeks passed, and the transformation revealed itself slowly – as if the building were testing the light after a long convalescence. The once-flaking façade now gleamed with the poise of something restored to itself. Crisp cornices reclaimed their edge, the etched fanlight shone like a freshly polished monocle, and the racing green front door – now resplendent – looked as though it might belong on the front row of an F1 grid or the cover of a heritage paint catalogue. The brass numberplate gleamed like a stage cue in the afternoon sun. Even the bellpull, though still disconnected, had been straightened and burnished to a defiant gleam, like an ageing actor ready for one final curtain call.

♪

It was a bright Saturday in the private garden, the rear of the building newly revitalised – its sash windows re-glossed, its ivy gently trimmed back. And the once-weary back door – newly painted, upright again, its proportions modestly dignified – now hung true on its hinges. Near this now-restored doorway, Lana appeared – arms folded, one eyebrow raised in faux-official inspection. Her mum followed behind, balancing a tray of potted herbs. I realised I'd known Lana for almost as long as I'd lived here – though I only noticed her properly once she emerged from the pram and began giving orders.

'That little glowing thing on your wall,' her mum began, gesturing casually towards my porch, 'what make of doorbell is that? Does it have one of those built-in cameras?'

'It's just a doorbell,' I said, offering a polite smile.

She nodded, looking satisfied. But before either of us could say anything else, Lana piped up brightly, 'That's what Smoky Pipe Man said it was! He said Mummy should ask because you always know about these things.'

Her mum gave a quick, embarrassed laugh and cast an awkward glance my way, as if trying to wave the moment off.

'Oh – he was just being funny,' she said, her voice breezy. 'Don't mind her.'

'Of course,' I said – though the moment lingered like a small cloud that refused to dissolve.

The exchange felt off-kilter. I had the distinct impression she wasn't asking for herself at all.

SUCH AN ODD WORD TO USE

Why? Something had interfered with my previous door-bell camera – and indeed the door-viewer before that. There had been the regular presence of shadowy figures at the front of the property, followed by those strange visits to the garden in the days leading up to the device's failure. And often, there seemed to be some subtle interaction between those visitors and Alistair.

My replacement doorbell had no visible markings to identify its make or model. That was something one would presumably need in order to take control of it. The scenes I had witnessed – Alistair standing with his back to my wall on either side of the doorbell – would have afforded him ample opportunity to confirm this fact at close quarters. Use of an intermediary to pose the direct question was a logical follow-up play.

At times, it felt as though I were caught up in an elaborate little game. Perhaps Alistair was reliving past experiences, indulging in a nostalgic sense of intrigue – or maybe I was simply overthinking a series of otherwise ordinary events.

Even so, he seemed to enjoy maintaining an air of control. 'Everything under control?', Alistair had asked that day from inside the hallway.

And yet, there was something theatrical in the way it all played out. Roles chosen, lines rehearsed, it was as if I'd wandered into a dress rehearsal for a play whose script I hadn't been given. As though the house – my house – wasn't the setting, but the stage itself.

Chapter 23

Lana's Map

It began with Lana asking a simple question from her upstairs window:

'Do you know how to draw rooftops from above?'

I was in the garden, trimming back a climbing vine. I shielded my eyes from the sun and looked up.

'Not especially,' I called back, 'but I imagine squares and rectangles are a good start.'

She gave a thoughtful nod. 'That's what I thought too.'

Only later would I realise this was part of a much larger undertaking – a hand-drawn, heavily annotated map of the neighbourhood, compiled by Lana over the course of a year. A map whose symbols, borders, and colour codes revealed more than one might expect from a child's drawing. It wasn't just a creative pastime – it was an act of deep, almost forensic observation.

I first saw the map properly one afternoon when her mum invited me over for tea. Lana greeted me at the door with paint-stained fingers and a conspiratorial look.

SUCH AN ODD WORD TO USE

'I've got something to show you,' she said, ushering me inside.

She led me to the dining table with the hushed reverence of a museum curator unveiling a lost tapestry. The paper – now far larger than the scraps I'd seen her working on in the garden, perhaps A2 and expanded with taped-on flaps – was spread across the table and anchored by the nearest objects to hand: a half-used scented candle, a cup of biros, an orphaned television remote, and a jar of unopened pickled beetroot. It was a brightly coloured patchwork of houses, trees, shaded paths, and figures whose names read like private riddles. But what immediately caught my eye was the level of detail.

'You're on here,' she said, tapping a rectangle shaded in grey-blue. 'That's your house. And that's the beanbag.'

'Of course,' I said. 'Can't forget the beanbag.'

She grinned, then pointed to a red squiggle and a series of loops. 'That's your terrace. You can tell because of the silver plant and the strange zapper.'

She had even included my window zapper, which she'd once watched me demonstrate. A tiny, dotted red line arced from my hand to an upper window – a laser trajectory terminating in a playful *ZAP!* labelled in silver pen. The alarming detail was a second dotted line that appeared to arc across the garden from behind a hash-patterned curtain.

Immediately below, on the wall near the communal gate, she had drawn a small pair of scissors – perfectly symmetrical, mid-snip – with a faint line trailing from either blade,

121

curling like ribbon down each side. The label beneath it read simply: *oops*. I glanced up from the map, and she was already grinning.

'I think that bit's classified,' she said, utterly serious. 'Same as where the biscuits go.'

Also close to the gate was the wood slatted garden bench. And there, beneath the bench – accurately positioned – was a tiny square marked with a question mark, surrounded by faint concentric lines, as if radiating mystery.

'That's where Mummy looked under the bench that time,' she said, matter-of-factly.

'I remember,' I replied, unsure whether to be amused or unnerved.

'She didn't know why she was doing it,' Lana added with a shrug. 'She just said someone asked.'

A little further down the path, not far from the shared bin store, was another figure – boldly drawn, with an exaggerated swirl of curly hair and cartoonishly bright yellow gloves. One hand held a sagging bin bag, the other pointed vaguely at nothing. The label read: *Bin Inspector (always appears after you've tidied)*.

I traced the rest of the map with my eyes. One corner showed the pavement outside. Parked half-on, half-off the kerb, was a black rectangle annotated: *mystery car – always goes after three minutes.*

A cluster of other street figures appeared too – some marked with single-word descriptions like *Looper, Recorder*

SUCH AN ODD WORD TO USE

and *Laughs-but-only-once.* She pointed to one called *Beanie Blinker.*

'He always walks past on Tuesdays. He blinks a lot but never talks.'

I blinked myself, unsure whether to laugh or start taking notes.

'Why are you keeping track of all this?' I asked, not unkindly.

She looked up. 'Because nobody else does.'

On the steps leading down from the green door was a stick figure girl with a big phone and large sunglasses. The label read: *pretends to talk but never says words.* I raised an eyebrow.

'She's always there when you're going out somewhere fancy,' Lana whispered, as if sharing a spy secret. 'But she doesn't say hello.'

A tiny icon of a watering can hung beside an uncannily accurate rendering of the communal path, complete with overhanging shrubbery sketched like spindly spider legs reaching over the wall, and a dotted line marking *the dark part where people disappear for a second.*

Then there was the real surprise. Right by my porch, where my potted herbs lived, was a character in a sun hat and gardening gloves – *plant lady*, the label read, with a note beneath it in slightly smudged biro: *only appears when you go on holiday.*

'I've never seen her,' I said.

123

'Well, she doesn't do much,' Lana replied. 'Just waters and tidies.'

I leaned closer. Outside my own front door, she had also drawn a stick figure in a trench coat with question marks for eyes. *He looks at the lights, not the door,* it read.

Right above the figure, she'd scribbled a tiny open window with a speech bubble that read only '. . . ?' – as though the house were thinking but not yet ready to speak.

I leaned back. For a moment I didn't know what to say. This wasn't a child's picture – it was a careful ledger of peculiar goings-on. A dossier of the mildly uncanny, lovingly rendered in Crayola and felt-tip.

'I think it's brilliant,' I said, and I meant it.

She smiled. 'I want to make a version in colour pencil next – this one's the prototype.'

I raised an eyebrow. *Prototype.* From the mouth of someone who still needed a step stool at the sink.

I stayed a little longer than I meant to. Her mum made tea – Lana darted in and out, offering explanations as she coloured. There was a small, mismatched comfort in it all – like finding an annotated copy of your life drawn by someone too young to know it might be sensitive. And maybe that was the point. Lana hadn't judged. She had simply noticed.

As I stood to leave, I gestured to the map and said, 'I should call you Shirley Holmes.'

She frowned. 'Who's that?'

SUCH AN ODD WORD TO USE

'Sherlock Holmes's cousin,' I said. 'Much better at spotting patterns – and fonder of coloured pens.'

She grinned. 'I like her already.'

Back home, I returned to the rooftop beanbag. The evening light had softened, painting long shadows across the deck. From here, the garden looked calm, uneventful – as it always did. But now I knew better. I had seen the map. And someone had been paying close attention all along.

Chapter 24

The Pendulum Swings

As the days shortened and the air began to cool I found myself confronted once again by a cluster of curious incidents. These clusters seemed to emerge after stretches of uneventful calm. I sometimes wondered if they were timed to catch me off guard or agitated into existence by minor neighbourly occurrences.

Indeed it was following a slightly heated group email exchange over some small matter of little consequence that a few new characters joined the cast. These were not 'befrienders'. I wasn't quite sure whether to term them 'spotters' or 'harassers'. Some were annoyingly persistent, so perhaps a mix of the two.

One Sunday morning, while heading to a recent regular haunt for breakfast, I noticed someone wearing wired earbuds walk purposefully past the entrance I was heading towards. He seemed to notice something in my general direction, then abruptly doubled back and dived into the very place he'd just passed.

As I climbed the stairs, I saw him kissing an unresponsive young woman awkwardly on the forehead before sitting opposite her at a small table. They looked like strangers forced to share the space – each secretly hoping the other would vanish.

I took my usual spot at a long window bench where, unusually, every alternate seat was already occupied. From my vantage point, I couldn't help but notice that the couple didn't exchange a single word. The man seemed to angle himself to keep an eye in my general direction. And as I left a little later, their steady gaze followed me.

The prior Friday brought a much stranger encounter.

At my customary hour one afternoon, I decided to drop by a coffee shop I infrequently visited. Strolling through a sleepy neighbouring street, I caught sight of another abruptly swivelling figure, phone in hand, off in the distance. Was I imagining it, or had this secluded spot become their favoured lookout – a perfect vantage over the fork from which all paths diverged?

On entering the road, I might find a woman with one foot propped on a low wall, tying her laces, it seemed, though her dark sunglasses were turned not towards her shoes but towards me – or a man perched languidly on the same wall with a bottled soft drink by his side, as if resting, though perhaps a little too alert – or another standing beside a bike, head bowed over a phone, until, after I passed, both body and bike shifted, as if discerning my direction – or, of course, a perfectly ordinary traffic warden, which didn't rule out anything either. If I retraced my steps moments later, they would all be gone, the street reset, the performance folded neatly away.

It was tempting to assign 'swivellers' to my ever-expanding troupe – an idle taxonomy that helped defuse the irritation of their suffocating presence. Their abrupt pirouettes brought to mind spinner dolphins (*Stenella longirostris*), known for their acrobatic leaps and mid-air turns. As spinners are to the wider *Delphinidae* family, so 'swivellers' might be to the 'spotters'. Still, I decided against formal induction – best not to overpopulate the cast.

At the coffee shop, I sat at a thin wooden bar facing the window with a latte and a slice of blueberry cake. Earbuds in place, I was absorbed in the third audiobook of the *Three-Body Problem* trilogy by Chinese author Cixin Liu. I'd been enthralled by the Netflix adaptation, which covered only the first book and snippets of the second and third. Knowing the wait for the larger concluding parts would be long, I had turned to the books. I was now deep into *Death's End*, the expansive and spellbinding finale that soared through higher

SUCH AN ODD WORD TO USE

dimensions and the quantum realm, grounded in speculative science and human longing.

The window offered a view of the bustling road, with pedestrians passing to and fro. On the opposite side, a few yards to my left, a cobbled alleyway cut into the residential area beyond.

At some point, a man emerged from the hushed alleyway. Dressed in worn, paint-splattered builder's attire, he held a phone in his hand as he crossed the clamorous road – curious, I thought – people looking to make a call usually move toward calm, not away from it. He then stood facing the road, just outside the coffee shop, slightly to my left, no more than three or four feet away, separated only by the windowpane.

Wearing neither headphones nor earbuds, he initially held the phone up to his face. Then he did something strange.

He lowered his arm fully, letting the phone hang from his outstretched fingers, and began to swing it gently and wilfully from side to side, like a pendulum. The phone's screen faced me as it traced slow arcs in the air. My first instinct, though I'm not sure why, was to glance at the path being traced on the pavement below.

The strange motion continued for perhaps a minute before he crossed back over the road and disappeared down the alley. Why go to all that trouble to do that? Then again, maybe it was no more than a compulsive tic – a meaningless motion I'd read too much into.

I carried on with my audiobook for about twenty minutes to finish the chapter. When I got up to leave, the man re-emerged from the alleyway.

As I walked along the pavement, he walked parallel to me on the other side of the road, a few steps behind. At the lights, I paused and crossed the road, positioning myself behind him. In swift response, he crossed too, then headed down a side street. When I drew level with the corner of that street, now on the opposite side, I saw him doubling back again seemingly to ensure he was no longer in front.

Needing some groceries, I ducked into a small local supermarket and then headed home.

I told myself it might have been random. But that strange, wilful motion lingered – like a whisper meant only for me. It wasn't the act itself that unsettled me, but the absence of any logical anchor. The worst of it was the inward spiral of not knowing, and the suspicion that perhaps I wasn't meant to know at all.

Then another possible lunchtime encounter occurred at one of my regular sandwich and coffee shops. Once again, I was seated on a stool at a bar facing the window, this time eating a ploughman's baguette.

A woman approached from my left, moving with an almost gliding grace. She held the microphone end of her phone to her lips, its screen turned towards the window. Eyes fixed ahead, she gradually slowed as she drew level with me, before coming to a languid halt. For about ten seconds, she remained there, the phone's front-facing camera perfectly – and uncomfortably – aligned with my face, no more than two feet away on the other side of the glass. It was as if she were recording a specimen in a terrarium – or maybe checking her reflection in selfie mode. I hated that I even had to wonder. Then, with the same slow, fluid motion, she drifted gently out of view – leaving behind a strange emptiness, like a held breath released.

There were times I wished these characters might wander into Lana's map. But they never did. Her observations favoured the gently peculiar, the whimsically persistent, but were shaped by the limits of her vantage point. And besides, I suspected the margins of her map were already full.

By now, I was venturing out less, choosing instead to focus on work – at least that is what I told myself. Looking back, I wonder if this too was a further deepening of the withdrawal.

On the next occasion I did go out – this time leaving my phone at home – yet another singular encounter. I visited a café I'd been to the two prior Saturdays at roughly the same time. I took a circuitous route via a hidden path known only to locals.

After getting there, and ordering from the counter, I grabbed a seat by the window. There were two people sat at a corner table, ideally positioned with a view of all other tables in the crowded café. And they kept glancing directly at me.

When I left, I noticed someone ahead of me taking photos of seemingly nothing in particular. They snapped a series of shots in a vaguely theatrical single, fluid movement – without pausing, framing, or focusing. The moment I walked past them, they began to follow.

I stopped and slowly crossed the road. Now, finding themselves ahead of me, they half-turned, as if trying to determine my position. Then they also crossed the road, appearing to try a little too hard to seem casual. Still a few yards in front, they suddenly darted down a side street, pivoted, and re-emerged behind me. For a moment I paused – less from alarm than a hollow kind of resignation. I felt like a character in someone else's rehearsal, one whose lines kept shifting.

I doubled back and went home via that same side street.

What on earth was this? A practice run for new recruits, confirming my routine in the process? Once confirmed, would the 'befrienders' again be wheeled in? Had they been instructed to be obvious on purpose, and if so, what would that achieve? Were they candidates for potential recruitment, and capturing a close-up image of me without my noticing would move them to the next round? My mind, starved of clarity, couldn't help filling in the blanks with theatrical nonsense. Was I now the invention test on the surveillance equivalent of *MasterChef*?

SUCH AN ODD WORD TO USE

I half-wondered if Lana had begun sketching a new symbol for her map – perhaps a small, fast-moving figure marked *Phone Dangler* or *Practises Walk-bys*. There might soon be no space left for shrubbery.

The following Saturday, after again taking the hidden path, I doubled back and went to a café in a different direction altogether. This time, I appeared to be free of any 'spotters'.

When I tried the same approach the Saturday after that, someone was dawdling halfway along the hidden path. They stood still, facing the bend in the trees, eyes cast off into the middle distance – as though awaiting a dog, or pretending to admire a view that didn't quite exist. There was something vaguely familiar about the way they held themselves. A sharp profile. A tilt of the head. I couldn't quite place them, but I felt certain I'd seen them before – perhaps seated near me once in a café, during one of those inexplicably clustered moments. And then they shifted slightly, turning just enough to avoid meeting my eyes – as if they too had remembered where they'd seen me. I wondered if they were there to confirm I'd actually passed through. So, I did go right through, then doubled back via an adjacent street and went to a random café.

Only randomness and leaving my phone behind seemed to keep the watchers at bay – real or imagined. But what I was really avoiding, I think, was the steady fraying of calm. Randomness, I'd discovered, had a strange way of restoring it. Routine would have to go. And perhaps that wasn't such a bad thing anyway. I found I tended to enjoy things more when they were spontaneous. Habits only offered disappointment when briefly interrupted. Spontaneity offered something more positive.

Over the years, there had been countless mysterious characters. There's no reason why they would question what they'd been asked to do. They must get live, or training, tasks all the time without having any inkling of the bigger picture. Only one person need know the true whys and wherefores. I even wondered if they themselves speculated about who they were watching and why. Watching me served no more purpose than following a squirrel in a nearby park. It seemed like such a waste of resources.

Another unsettling occurrence was a food delivery – if indeed that was what it was.

Having finished drying myself off after a shower, and wearing a hooded towelling robe, I set about removing the moisture from the tiles, first with a scraper, then an absorbent cloth. This was my latest strategy to defeat that orange residue, and it was an invigorating bit of extra daily exercise.

The doorbell rang. It was dusk. I was not expecting anyone and had no intention of answering in a bathrobe. I could see a figure at the door. They wore all-black biker gear, including a black helmet with a blacked-out visor. A small bright light jutted out from atop the helmet, and for a few moments they stood on the porch step with the helmet almost pressed against the door.

After ringing the bell three times, the figure stood back a little and hung around. I could see they were holding a handled brown paper bag barely large enough for a sandwich.

I often took food deliveries from nearby restaurants, so I was quite familiar with the normal appearance and behaviour of delivery drivers. Aside from the wrong address, there were several things that seemed somewhat unusual in this particular instance. There was no branding on the bag or anywhere on the outfit. There was no attempt to call the number of the person who placed the order, nor was there any contact with the restaurant to query where they had been sent.

At one point, the figure appeared to have gone, and I thought little more of it.

The next morning, one of the neighbouring tenants mentioned that the figure had lingered for several minutes with their back to my wall, appearing to stare at the window across the garden. I began to wonder whether their focus had truly been that window – or, more precisely, the reflection it held: the door they had studied so intently only moments earlier.

Perhaps it really was just a simple mixed-up delivery.

How do I deal with this? I can't wait it out – it's still happening long after the complaint. I can't simply ignore it – it nearly cost me my house. I tried the tribunal, but they dismissed my case. Much of the activity might be hard to prove, and discussing it with anyone could risk either appearing paranoid or allowing snippets of information to find an innocent path back to the person in control. Sharing too much might unwittingly help refine the methods of whoever might be behind these peculiar occurrences, if indeed they are intentional. And I still wasn't certain. Perhaps they want to provoke a reaction. Any reaction might appear frivolous in the absence of compelling evidence. Then it looks like the problem is me.

In the end, I did what I always do when the outside world becomes too uncertain – I reached for something quieter, something I could hold.

It wasn't until I sat down with a book that my thoughts finally began to settle – and, ironically, it was that book that lured one of them back.

Chapter 25

The Fog Lifts

While reading one evening, I stumbled across a phrase that snagged at me: *an underhand planning application.* I'd heard it before, drifting from Alistair's open window months earlier. I'd dismissed it at the time – after all, I'd only been exploring an idea encouraged by Planning, nothing submitted. It was one of many paranoid ideas I was trying to let go of. But the word still caught me. Underhand. As if I'd done something furtive or hidden, when all I had ever done was apply – openly, properly, by the book.

Maybe I was reading too much into it. Maybe not.

A few days later, I ran into Lana in the garden. She was crouched beneath the overhang of the fig tree with a clipboard balanced on her knees, using a black crayon to trace bold outlines. At her side sat a tin of mismatched pens, chalk, and a single silver paint marker that had clearly seen better days.

'New map update?' I asked, trying not to hover too obviously.

She shook her head. 'This one's a study. I'm trying to fit in the new man. The one with the paper bag. But there isn't really space.'

She looked up at me with that same measuring squint I'd seen before, as if assessing how much to share.

'He doesn't come very often,' she added. 'But he talks to the door like it's listening.'

I paused. 'Which door?'

She shrugged. 'Yours. I think he wants it to reply.'

She tapped a blank patch at the edge of the paper, beneath a row of stick figures. I caught a glimpse of a strange new character added in pencil – someone wearing what appeared to be a helmet, with a bright light above the head and two words scrawled beneath it: *Still trying*.

I was about to ask more, but her mum called out from the kitchen, and Lana darted off without another word, the clipboard tucked under her arm.

Back inside, I tried to forget the conversation, but that sketch stayed with me. The figure. The light. The odd comment about the door – and that caption, as if the door itself were the one resisting.

SUCH AN ODD WORD TO USE

And then came the slip of paper carelessly dropped by one of those recently encountered characters. I saw it flutter gently to the ground unnoticed by anyone else. I scooped it up and walked on without giving it a second glance. Once home, I was able to examine it.

At some point, the left side had clearly been damp. The first jotted mark was illegible. The second was the upper-case name of the coffee shop I had visited only moments before. The second line was what appeared to be a telephone number. All but the last part was smeared. But those final four digits looked somehow familiar.

I remembered two large boxes, carelessly left by a delivery driver inside the side path – the labels had caught my eye. The boxes were so large that they left no room to pass. I had to stop and stack them out of view of the street. Only by reading the labels, addressed to Alistair as it turned out, did I know where best to leave them. At the time I noticed that the final four digits of the contact number were very close to corresponding to one of my streaming-service PIN numbers. A single digit only needed incrementing by one. But which digit had been the anomaly? And why did it now feel significant?

I couldn't help but reflect on the improbability of those final four digits on the slip of paper matching the ones on the box label – it would be something like one in ten thousand. Add that to the name of the coffee shop I'd left only moments earlier? Well, perhaps I was seeing what I wanted to see – seeking meaning in a coincidence because so little else made sense. There's a fine line between pattern recognition and wishful thinking – and I was always walking it.

Even if I had been certain that the numbers matched, there must be something like one hundred million active telephone numbers in the UK. That would mean ten thousand matching those final four digits. And anyway, only I knew the provenance of that slip of paper. Without a proper chain of custody, it was heartening, but no more than that.

Yet coincidences gather like threads – loose, aimless – until one more slips into place and a pattern emerges: a rug too intricate for accident. My sanity felt closer to being restored. But still no way out.

In a book, film or TV series, all the pieces would be falling into place to reveal a single satisfying truth. My pieces simply left me with glimpses of something shifting behind a thick blanket of London fog. Weird clusters of cyphers and hard-to-prove, hard-to-explain stifling surveillance.

I had grown increasingly weary. It was difficult to see how to break free. Perhaps I could not.

Had it been a stalker, there might have been emails, phone calls, text messages, or the repeated presence of an individual who could be identified – an image captured, preserved, reduced to an array of pixels. But this was something else entirely. It felt more akin to those ghost-like particles of nature that bombard us constantly yet leave no trace.

I wrestled with what I had done to warrant this. I was a considerate neighbour. I improved my home, as countless

SUCH AN ODD WORD TO USE

others do. I caused no disturbance – neither using the terrace at night, nor during the day in any way that could be considered intrusive. My outside spaces were clean, well-kept. My presence was unassuming. And yet, it seemed that simply improving my home was enough to stoke the ire and draw the heat of a neighbour – one with a rather unusual background, not typically found living next door.

I always thought that people with such backgrounds would dissolve into the shadows.

Chapter 26

Curtain Call

But one last piece was about to fall into place, revealing that elusive, singular, satisfying truth. Something in me had stirred – as if a long-guarded position had quietly uncoiled, a defensive line giving way not to collapse but to revelation – one nocturnal insectivore shape-shifting into another. A clarity began to surface, slow and deliberate, as if the endgame had already begun, and I was only now noticing – teasing apart the threads of that enigmatic Filofax. Names hidden in cyphers. Dates. Yet no clue as to where the individuals behind those names might be found or what they had in common. The lettered tabs seemed to offer a silent map – each set of names pointing to a particular location, the volume under each tab suggesting its importance.

Positing that the surveillance and cyphers were somehow linked, I considered where Britain's security apparatus might have focused its efforts at that Cold War inflection point. Moscow, as the heart of the Soviet Union at the time, would surely have been a top priority for intelligence

SUCH AN ODD WORD TO USE

gathering during the Cold War and its immediate aftermath. The hefty sheaf of pages under M seemed entirely consistent with that notion.

The first decoded name under M was Lucas Tremblay – likely French Canadian, as Tremblay was common in Quebec. Nathan Reid had the ring of an English-speaking Canadian, possibly from Nova Scotia. And given Canada's significant South Asian immigrant population – particularly in British Columbia and Ontario – Alina Singh could easily pass as a bilingual Indo-Canadian.

All three would be perfect for Non-Official Cover identities: fabricated personas tied to neutral nationalities, designed to avoid drawing undue attention. Private individuals with no overt connections to the UK government, taking enormous risks without the safety net of diplomatic protection if discovered.

In those days, Berlin in West Germany would surely have been a key focal point of Cold War tensions, especially during Germany's reunification in 1990. As a city divided between East and West, it was a nexus of espionage and intelligence operations. Beijing, reflecting China's growing global influence and its delicate balancing act between the Soviet Union and the West, would also have been a priority. Then Baghdad – around the time of the 1990–91 Gulf War under Saddam Hussein – emerged as a major focus for Western intelligence. It seemed no coincidence that B was the second-heaviest section of the notebook.

That left other plausible contenders. Washington was a critical ally. London served as the nerve centre for managing global networks. Kabul grappled with the vacuum left by the 1979–89 Soviet–Afghan War. Paris was a major Western power and a hub of European politics and commerce. And Havana remained a key Soviet ally in the Western Hemisphere, retaining strategic importance even as the Cold War waned.

Then there were T, N, and J. Tehran stood out as a crucial location for monitoring Middle Eastern developments, particularly after the 1979 revolution and amid Iran's strained relations with the West. New Delhi, given India's non-aligned stance and its strategic position between the Soviet Union and the West, was another likely candidate. Finally, Johannesburg – during South Africa's transition away from apartheid and its broader role in African geopolitics – would have been of great interest to the intelligence community.

I grew increasingly confident that this was a compilation of agent cover names, organised by assigned location. But why on earth such a thing would be hidden away in my bathroom wall made no sense at all.

Over the next two weeks, I set other distractions aside and returned to the specialised music archives, official artist biographies, and studio records, this time on the hunt for session dates. Aside from the famous rock bands – Zinc

SUCH AN ODD WORD TO USE

Void, Deep Mauve, Lead Balloon, and Blind Bobcat – a lesser-known group now captured my attention. Desert Penguins had sessions conveniently aligning with each of the five distinct dates found in the Filofax, generally about two weeks later. Even more intriguingly, they performed gigs either in Russia or in cities with strong Soviet sympathies within a month of those sessions.

I recalled the newspaper clipping about the disappearance of Viktor Ralston, the studio's bookings administrator. It reported that he vanished 'shortly after the recent recording sessions of Zinc Void and Desert Penguins.' It appeared, in fact, to be after the very last known session of the Penguins.

His first name had a faintly Eastern European ring to it – subtle enough not to stand out in a cosmopolitan city. Ralston, by contrast, sounded anglicised, perhaps adapted to help him blend seamlessly into British society. In the clipping, colleagues described him as 'incredibly hard-working – often arriving long before anyone else and leaving long after.' In light of everything I'd now uncovered, I couldn't help seeing that remark through an entirely different lens.

Had I dug out a mole hibernating on the other side of the garden? Perhaps Alistair's obsession had never truly been with me, nor with the improvements to my house *per se* – it was a concern for something burrowed deep within.

Maybe I should have paid more attention when George Smiley crept into my thoughts – that quiet mental nudge I'd mistaken for overthinking.

I could see now that the Filofax likely belonged to Alistair, its contents carefully and meticulously compiled during his tenure at the Cabinet Office, liaising with the agencies whose names were seldom spoken outside closed rooms. A short scurry across a private garden runway, hidden from prying eyes, enabled the covert passing of intelligence to Viktor, whom I now deduced to be his KGB handler. These visits to the studio, several days before the Penguins' recording sessions, provided the perfect recreational cover.

I recalled the first time I met Alistair, years earlier, when he had been disturbed by the flickering light. What came to mind was the wistful way he spoke of the recording studio, his gaze lingering on the blank porch wall where its sign had presumably once hung. Those intimate sessions with Zinc Void *et al.* may have fuelled his nostalgia, but I suspect his deeper longing was for the thrill of the great game – a game once played within the very walls of my home.

With that recollection came the pungent aroma of oak-cured pipe tobacco rising from a smouldering bowl carved from rich, dark wood. Holding the Filofax beneath my nose, I caught the same faint yet unmistakable trace of that tobacco, nearly lost beneath the heavier scent of aged leather.

In many ways, the precise details of the tradecraft employed were of little matter. Only Viktor, as the man in the middle, would be privy to all the steps. Yet I initially puzzled over why the notebook was still here at all. Thinking through a plausible sequence of events helped resolve that conundrum.

SUCH AN ODD WORD TO USE

Alistair and the nameless Penguin – whom I shall now playfully call Rockhopper – could never meet. Perhaps Viktor invited Alistair to listen to a recording session with a different band, one scheduled a few days earlier. Records showed this was one of two such bands, creating the appearance of a genuine liking for their music. This could have been Alistair's opportunity to deliver the latest cyphers and retreat to his country residence, thus putting both time and distance between himself and Rockhopper.

While the Penguins hammered out fresh riffs on reel-to-reel tape, Viktor, carefully mimicking Rockhopper's handwriting, might have transcribed the latest staves into intentionally blank spaces in his personal manuscript book. A small note could have subtly indicated the intended city. For instance, after penning three Moscow staves, he might have crossed them out and scribbled 'Muddled' in the margin.

Rejected, discordant snippets lost in a crowd of real experimentation – written in the same apparent hand – ensured that nothing would draw undue attention to Rockhopper on his later travels.

Once the Penguins departed, Viktor could have reunited these pages with the Filofax and replaced the tiling – both concealing the cyphers and ensuring a backup in case anything went awry. Perhaps, too, it was intended as a form of personal insurance – though if so, it may not have been enough.

A similar line of thinking must have occurred to Alistair.

Why Viktor disappeared remains a matter of speculation. Perhaps he had outlived his usefulness, and the KGB had no intention of leaving a loose end. Alistair, however, could never be certain whether any record of his treachery had been left behind. He had likely scoured the property prior to my purchase but fully dismantling it would have been out of the question. For Alistair, even the mere suggestion of a planner, builder, or roofer on the premises would have signalled a code red.

If I sold my house to someone beyond his sphere of monitoring, it would mean rebuilding the entire system of surveillance on some new pretext – determining the new owner's routine, or possibly multiple owners' and, heaven forbid, finding they prefer a knocker to a doorbell. What's more, those new owners might have been more inclined to make major alterations.

If something hidden were ever unearthed – by me or anyone else – Alistair had to be the first to know, so he could *control* the situation before it spiralled out of hand.

Had I been almost anyone else, that strategy might have worked. Few people are as content as I am with a life of minimal interaction. Most others would have produced vital early intelligence through casual remarks or discarded scribbled notes. But with me, there was so little to work with. I had told no one, for instance, about discovering the mysterious cyphers.

All that remained now was to take everything to the police and let them decide whom to involve. After that, I could

SUCH AN ODD WORD TO USE

return to my work with a renewed fixity of purpose. It was for others to decide whether the truth should out.

I heard no more on the matter. What I can say is that I never again saw any of those peculiar characters: no 'scanners', no 'planters' or 'retrievers', no 'spotters' and no 'befrienders'.

For a moment, I even considered suggesting to Lana that she add one final creature to her map – a small, cautious blur darting between doorways, nose twitching at the air, always just out of reach. She'd need a new label, of course. Perhaps *Scurrier* would do, or *Doorstep Sniff*, or simply *???*. I imagined her nodding solemnly and pencilling it in right below the watering can and the trench coat man – another presence that didn't quite belong, yet somehow made perfect sense.

The curtain fell on the long-running show. I stepped out into daylight – free of cues, free of cast. The air felt refreshingly clear and abundant.

Until I glanced back.

His kitchen blinds were drawn again. Not closed. Not open. Simply drawn – tilted just enough to see without being seen. A bristle still raised. And somewhere, perhaps in the far corner of Lana's ever-growing map, Scurrier still watched.

The End

Acknowledgements

My thanks first to Zoila Marenco and Kiana Palombo at Whitefox – to Zoila for warmly inviting me into their publishing world, and to Kiana, my project editor, for deftly steering me through it, keeping everything moving and offering generous advice at every stage.

I'm also grateful to Gill Phillips (Reviewed & Cleared) for her clear and thoughtful legal advice; Peter Salmon for his insightful structural edit; Kay Coleman and Emily Reader for their meticulous edits; Dan Mogford for a bold cover design that evokes a sense of intrigue; Typo•glyphix for their typesetting services; and Jess King for delivering a comprehensive and considered marketing campaign.

About the author

Carl Goodwin is a London-based author. With a background in data science and strategy, he writes quietly unsettling fiction exploring the intersections of psychology, systems and the stories we tell ourselves.